Blue Water Bedlam

Four Retired Guys
...a Newish Yacht
...a Boatload of Trouble

Barry Sanders – writing as:

B. G. Preston

Blue Water Bedlam

This is a work of fiction. Names, characters, places and events are a product of the author's imagination. Any resemblance to actual persons, living or dead, business establishments or locales is entirely coincidental.

@ Cover Art by Cora Graphics

ISBN-13: 978-0-9861477-5-3

First Edition: August 2015

Updated: March 2019

www.BGPreston.com

Other Works by B.G. Preston

Camino Passages

The Camino de Santiago is a wonderful historical trail across northern Spain which provides hikers with an incredible variety of natural and cultural delights. It also, as Larry Adams learns, is a social journey as well.

After his wife's untimely death, Larry sets out for a solo adventure and a much-needed change of pace. What he encounters during his walk are experiences and new relationships which could change his life forever. Along the way, he meets a charming woman from France. Together, they visit many villages, towns, and natural features which enrich their understanding of this beautiful region and each other.

Camino Passages, written by the author of the successful *Camino Easy* guide to the Camino Frances, is a work of fiction, but one which is rich in description and relationships. Anyone who enjoys adventure fiction and stories of travel will enjoy Camino Passages.

Acknowledgments

For Sandra, thank you for your patience and support as I spent many hours in my study working on this book. I can now come out and actually communicate a bit.

To "the Rohnert Park Guys"…the idea for this story indirectly came from you.

This work was professionally edited by Donna Nicely. Her guidance and input have helped significantly and has greatly improved the quality of this work.

Maps and diagrams were completed by Rachel L. Walker. Her attention to detail was greatly appreciated.

Thank you also to Cora Graphics for the great work done in crafting the cover for this work and other works by B.G. Preston.

Murphy's Law...

*"Anything that can go wrong...
will go wrong."*

Modern version

1: Four Guys Walk Into a Bar

The day began normally; it just didn't stay that way.

By the end of the day, the anticipation of a new adventure — and some added excitement — was foremost on my mind. It was just that little bit about a murder that put an unfortunate twist to it all.

Thursday morning. I was the last of our little group to enter the coffee bar. The other three were already there. McDuck's Coffee Bar was across from a large marina in our little Puget Sound town of Anacortes, Washington. The owner, Mac — with no apparent last name — was a friend of sorts. Otherwise, we probably would not have gone there. McDuck's was a mashup of an old Denney's, with a hint of a greasy donut shop, combined with the aroma of last year's burnt coffee.

I had to chuckle as I walked in, only to see a middle-aged couple turn and leave after just barely stepping inside and shaking their heads in dismay. McDuck's was definitely not their kind of place. Bad for them, good for the four of us.

One great thing about McDuck's was the view of the marina where we could watch the yachts and fishing boats come and go. Starbucks, located down the road in a strip mall, didn't have this view. They just had better, well, almost everything. Just not the view.

McDuck's, off-putting atmosphere and all, was now our regular Thursday morning haunt. We had tried other places, but none of them had the no-one-cares-what-we-do-or-say-there ambiance, so McDuck's was it. We were all retired and our routine had somehow evolved into getting together once a week and, McDuck's was now our default place.

Okay, the tourists might not want anything to do with the place, but in a town which was often overrun with tourists and their RVs and their heads-down-devoted to their smart phones approach, it was a relief to be able to go to a place which we just about claim as our own.

Coming to McDuck's was also the one and only regular thing on our schedules. By the way, the term "regular," for a group of retirees, takes on a whole variety of meanings, but we won't go there.

Two retired cops, a retired firefighter and a retired marketing guy, me. Once a week we came into the bar…the coffee bar. Real bars had little interest anymore.

The three other guys knew each other from their previous careers. I was the interloper, having only joined the group through the good fortune of Scott's and my wives knowing each other. During our sessions there at McDuck's I totally enjoyed listing to their retelling of past cases, fires and crimes they had worked on. Oddly enough, they showed little interest in my describing the wonderful Excel spreadsheets I had created as a marketing guy.

"Hey, Frank, I have great news!" Charlie gleefully called out as I strolled toward the counter and past the booth where the others sat, a large four-person booth near the front window. This one window was kept clean…by us. The other windows were coated a light brown. We liked the view but knew waiting for Mac to clean the windows was probably futile, so we kept this one relatively clean.

"Can't wait to hear," I replied while focusing on my upcoming order, and not on him. "Tell me more, right after I get my coffee plus some of those brown things."

"McBeignets!" Scott, the tall, retired cop from Everett, exclaimed in reference to my "brown thing" comment.

"Is that what they are? I'll be damned. Couldn't quite tell by looking at them," I answered, stating an overused joke among us. I went up to Mac, as he stood there with his huge belly pushing out against his stained apron, while giving me his usual impatient look.

Another great thing about this place was the McBeignet. Mac had invented and made them himself. These were the brown things I was referring to. McBeignets are sort of a mix of a New Orleans beignet, a croissant, plus something else I couldn't identify. In appearance, they are lumpy, a bit orange-brown in color and totally unappealing. The thing is, they are absolutely delicious. I had had beignets when visiting New Orleans a few years back, but Mac's morphed version of croissant-thingy-beignet outdid them.

"You ought to patent these things or something," I said to Mac for the hundredth time as I stood across from him at the cluttered counter to place my order.

You used to be able to get table service in McDuck's. Not anymore. Mac took a lesson from Starbucks...don't go to where the customer is sitting, have the customer come to you, and then double the price. It worked. Almost, anyway. The minimal number of customers was a sure indicator that Starbucks was still winning the popularity contest.

With one hand grasping a hot mug of coffee, I headed toward the group who were sitting in our special, cleaned-by-us booth, an old Formica table showing years of wear, along with the bench seats that had long since lost any semblance of comfort.

I had ordered a Duzy-size coffee. Mac had figured if Starbucks could name all sizes of their drinks in words meaning large or big — Vente, Grande, Tall — so could he. Mac said Duzy was Polish for large. I'd never looked it up to confirm, having just taken him at his word for it. In my other hand, I had a small plastic basket with a dozen McBeignets. I only needed three for me. The rest, I knew, would quickly be consumed by the others at the booth.

I sat on the lumpy, in-need-of-repair vinyl bench seat next to Dawn. She was our fourth "guy". Dawn was a retired police detective and, like Scott, had served in Everett, a town an hour south of us where the two of them had come to know and respect each other. Despite her shape being a bit different from the rest of us, she was definitely one of the guys. Any attempts to treat her any differently from the rest of us typically went south. The built-like-guys guys had long ago stopped trying to be careful about the nature of our jokes around her as we had all learned that she could fire back verbal missiles equal to or better than anything we could come up with.

So, the four of us sat there, about to hear more of Charlie's announcement. Our little group consisted of: Dawn, our divorced, female retired detective; Scott, the semi-balding, married and retired cop from Everett; me, a retired married, marketing guy, previously from Ohio; and our fourth member, Charlie, was a retired fireman who had been a widower for over a year. The other notable fact about Charlie was that he was a lotto winner. According to Charlie, per the good graces of the Washington State Lottery, he was now about thirty million, after taxes, richer.

We all liked Charlie.

~ ~ ~ ~ ~ ~

2: I Bought a Boat

"So, what's this great news, Charlie? Or, do you prefer to drag it out and delay coming to the point like you usually do?" I playfully taunted him as I blew on my hot coffee, waiting for it to cool down. Mac always brewed his coffee way too hot, and Charlie rarely came to a point in his stories.

"He has been squirmy just waiting for us all to get here so he can tell us," Dawn said in assessment of our friend, who sat across the worn table.

"Can it be any greater than when you won the lottery?" Scott asked him. He was the only one of the group who had been openly envious of Charlie's good fortune, the rest of us just enjoyed the benefits of Charlie's good fortune. Charlie had been great to us. A few months back he had taken me, Scott, Dawn, and Scott's and my wives on a cruise to Alaska. He had also purchased new cars for each of us.

Like I said, we all liked Charlie.

"I know!" Dawn announced. "I can tell by the look on his face. My ex, the skunk-bastard, used to have that same look right after he would get lucky with some twenty-something coed." Dawn's husband had been an instructor at a community college. Late in the game, Dawn had learned he had a special, up-close-and-personal way of tutoring the young coeds. After learning of this, and as a former detective, she openly kicked herself for not noticing the signs. She looked Charlie over and firmly pronounced, "You got lucky, yourself. Didn't you?"

I looked over at Charlie. As much as I liked him as a friend, and enjoyed his quick but goofy wit, I couldn't imagine him ever getting lucky. At least, not in that special guy-meets-girl sort of way. He'd probably been a handsome guy once. Now, though, Charlie was simply dumpy. Not necessarily fat, just rumpled, haggard and unkempt looking. Ever since his wife had died, he had stopped giving much attention to his own personal care and feeding and it showed.

"Nah, it has to be something else," I teased. "No respectable female would have you." I had to be careful with teasing Charlie. While we all took playful jabs at one another, we did occasionally overdo it, especially with Charlie. More than once we had bruised his ego. Still, that didn't slow us down much.

Now, he sat there looking at us with a big grin on his face. Without saying anything, he reached into a bag that was sitting on the cracked-vinyl seat beside him. Ever so slowly, and with a bit of fanfare on his part, Charlie pulled out a hat. It was a white cloth hat with a shiny black bill. The front was adorned with a bit of gold braid sporting some sort of emblem on it. He placed it on his head, enabling us to see what the emblem was. A symbol of a gold-on-black crest with the word "Captain" embossed below it.

"What the hell is that?" Scott growled. "Looks like some sort of pretend captain's cap or something!"

"Play nice, Scott," Dawn pretended to scold him, and then took her own turn to play with Charlie. "It looks more like the hat a tour guide would wear at *Sea World*," she twisted Scott's comments even further.

"Really, Charlie, what is this?" I asked.

"It is a captain's cap. I bought a boat, and I'm the captain!" He exclaimed proudly as he reached down into the bag, bringing out three more similar caps. He handed one to each of us. They all had the title of "Co-Captain" embossed on them.

"Whoa!" Dawn exclaimed. "First, what the hell is this about a boat, and second, what is with this co-captain thing? There is no such title in boating that I know of!"

"There isn't?" Charlie looked bewildered.

"Skip the hats for now," I interrupted. "What's this about a boat?"

Before answering our questions, he looked down at one of the caps he had put on the table before us. Charlie was obviously smarting from learning there was no such title as co-captain. "I had those hats made special for you guys. That sucks! You'd have thought the guy at the hat store would have said something."

"Enough about the damn hats, Charlie," Dawn interjected. "Like Frank said, what's this about a boat?"

Charlie, happy to turn the conversation away from the oddly labeled hats, gleefully looked at the three of us. "My cousin, a couple times removed, had owned it. He died a few months after getting it new, so his wife wanted to get rid of it. She said the boat had been bad luck for them. Given the way he died, she is probably right. Anyway, I looked into it, and talked to the guys down at the ship's store." He referenced the large place along the far side of the marina from where we sat. "They said it was a real bargain. So, I bought it!"

We all sat there, staring at Charlie. We didn't know what to say. I munched on a McBeignet while I mulled this over.

"So," Charlie went back to the topic of the hats, "if there aren't co-captains, what do you call the guys who help the captain? I want for you all to be part of my crew."

"We're your crew now?" I taunted playfully, taking care to not spit out my coffee as I gasped in surprise.

"Hush, play nice," Dawn said as she nudged me.

"I don't know, Charlie," Scott joined in a bit belatedly as he tried to answer Charlie's question about the actual titles for a co-captain. "I think they are called First Mate or something similar."

"There is no way in hell I will be First Mate to Charlie or any of you guys!" Dawn exclaimed.

"It's just a boat-crew title, not a late-night activity! Get a grip, already!" Scott retorted, then quickly turned away from the likely death-stare Dawn was so good at giving with her deep blue eyes.

"Hey, Charlie?" I asked, waiting to ensure I had his attention. "You get seasick, remember? Hell, when we were all on that Alaska cruise, you hurled your guts out. A lot."

"He did, didn't he," Scott laughed.

"Well, my new boat is supposed to have a stabilizer thing, so it won't rock much."

"And, you don't think the big-ass cruise ship we were on wasn't stable? It was probably way more solid on the water than your little boat ever will ever be!" I added, still not believing what I was hearing from Charlie.

Dawn, giving Scott and I a look only a woman knows how to do, finally got us to stop taking verbal prods at him. It was time to hear about Charlie's boat.

~ ~ ~ ~ ~ ~

3: Trixie's Destiny

Charlie, thoroughly deflated, just sat silently for a bit. I felt horrible. Well, maybe not horrible, but I knew we had gone too far. Here he was, beaming with pride about his new boat, while all we could do was ridicule him.

It actually had been rather fun.

"Tell us about your boat, Charlie," Dawn encouraged him. "We really want to know."

"No, you don't. You just want to be shits," he complained.

"We do...want to know about your boat, that is," I stated, trying to absolve the guilt I had from ridiculing him.

"You're still shits," he responded, but I could tell from the gleam in his eye that he was a bit appeased.

"Like you don't throw verbal bombs at us whenever we give you an opening!" Scott exclaimed. "Tell us about your stupid boat already!"

"Right after I finish my coffee," he replied, a bit petulant, trying to punish us by holding back on further information as he slowly sipped at his half-finished coffee. His was a Veliki size. I had yet to look up the term to find out what language for large Veliki is.

Finally, after several minutes, he stood from the booth and started toward the exit door as the rest of our little group sat there and watched him. "Well, instead of telling you about my boat, how about if I show you?" He nodded toward the neighboring marina. "It's over there."

"Do we have to wear these stupid hats?" Scott exclaimed as he followed along. This comment was soon followed by a slap to the back of his head from Dawn. "Sum bitch! Cut that out," Scott complained. This wasn't his first back-of-the-head slap from her. She loved to play like the character Gibbs on *NCIS*, who frequently gave these little slaps to another of the characters in the show. We had all been on the receiving end of these jabs from her. None of us dared to return the favor.

It was drizzling. It's often drizzling around here, so this didn't stop us from heading outside and over to the marina entrance a short, but wet, walk across a nearly empty parking lot. Living just about anywhere in the Puget Sound, you quickly became accustomed to gray skies with lots of drizzle and rain. Just like it was now. It was either get used to the wet climate or pack up your stuff and move to Phoenix or Florida. My wife and I had retired from Ohio, anxious to leave the depressingly gray winters there.

Somehow, we ended up in the Puget Sound. Far prettier than Ohio, but no improvement in the gray sky thing.

Charlie, wearing his new captain's cap with the rest of us wearing our co-captain's caps, strolled toward the entrance to the marina. The main gate was locked as usual, just as it should be. This didn't stop Charlie. He proudly leaned down to the keypad, entered the combination, and then swung open the chain-link metal gate.

"Ah, it would seem that he now is in possession of the secret code," I stated the obvious.

"Does your little boat at least have a bathroom? I really, really have to pee!" Dawn declared.

"They are called heads, not bathrooms," Charlie self-importantly explained. Now that he was a boat owner, I could see he was primed and ready to regale us with his knowledge of boating. If my guess was correct, other than knowing what to call a toilet, that knowledge was close to zero. More than the rest of us, maybe, but that wasn't saying much. Actually, I probably knew more than they did as I had read quite a bit on the topic. No practical knowledge, just a lot of wishful thinking and online brochure browsing.

"Why didn't you go before we left McDuck's Coffee Bar?" Scott complained to Dawn.

"Like I knew our impetuous friend here," she nodded toward Charlie, "was going to suddenly dart out the door. A little warning would be nice."

The Cap Sante Marina is one of the largest boating facilities on Fidalgo Island. This particular marina is huge, and home to hundreds of boats of all types. To me, it was a source of endless fascination.

As we strolled up one long, fifteen-foot wide, floating concrete pad, we passed numerous boats in their slips on either side of us. Many of the boats were sleek sailboats ranging anywhere from thirty to fifty feet in length. Intermixed with the sailboats with their towering masts, were powerboats of all sizes and shapes. I had often fantasized about having a boat and docking it here. My wife had other opinions on the subject, so...no boat.

Charlie's boat was apparently one of these along the dock we were on. Some were bright and new. Others were old and decrepit. Who knew what it was Charlie had bought into. He paused for a moment; I assumed from his stance that the thirty-two foot Sea Ray express yacht to our right might be his. It wasn't. Charlie had only paused to make sure we were keeping up.

"Where the hell is your little boat, Charlie?" Scott complained. "Couldn't you have parked the damn thing closer?"

"There isn't room for it closer in."

"Isn't room for it?" Dawn asked. "Charlie, my friend, just exactly what did you buy?"

"You'll see," he said with a touch of humor in his voice. Charlie was having fun toying with us.

We walked past several more boat slips. Finally, Charlie stopped, turned toward us, and looked toward his left. I looked in that direction and saw an old ketch, about fifty foot long, which was probably in its prime when Nixon was President. What had once been a fun vessel for a sailing adventure was now little more than a rest stop for sea gulls to poop onto. There was loads of the stuff on the boat.

"Charlie, you didn't!" Dawn exclaimed as she looked down on the wreck of a boat. "And, you can't possibly expect us to get in that thing, can you?"

He waited patiently for us to wind down while giving us a broad grin. He had been full of them today – a good thing, and I was glad to see him so happy. Since his wife, Glenda, had died, his spirits seemed to have largely gone, so if a crappy sailboat was what it was going to take to cheer him up, then so be it. I still wasn't sure how I felt about stepping aboard the horrible, seagull-poop-encrusted thing.

"You do know you have lots of money and can do better, right?" Scott announced as he looked with disdain at the boat just as a pair of seagulls landed in the aft cockpit, only to unleash a white gloppy mess of bird poop. A cockpit is the open area near the rear of a sailboat where people sit, steer the boat or just relax. In this case, it was also a place for layer upon layer of seagull crap to mound up.

"Yes, I can. I can do much better. Ta da!" He made a show of turning to face the end of the pier where a large white-hulled boat sat along the t-shaped end, blocking our view of the harbor with its seawall beyond.

"Where?" I asked, not tuning into what Charlie was trying to show us. "All I see is a big-ass yacht that some guy with more money than he knows what to do with would buy." Then it hit me. That description fit Charlie.

"That would be me. The guy with the big-ass yacht and more money than he knows what to do with," Charlie responded gleefully.

"Holy crap!" Scott proclaimed as he walked toward the large yacht, his mouth practically hanging open in amazement. "This is yours?"

"Yep," Charlie said simply.

"It's freaking huge. Beautiful, but super big!" Dawn added, trying to push back her shoulder-length, ash-gray hair as the damp sea breeze blew it around.

"You bought this?" I asked, not believing what I was seeing.

Before us was a new looking, Grand Banks motor yacht. This type of yacht was not the sleek Italian boat of my fantasies, but it was incredible, nonetheless. It was a practical-looking vessel, designed for long-range cruising at decent speeds, and built more for comfort and stability than speed or showmanship. I had studied the Grand Bank's website back when I dreamed of having a yacht. As a result, I knew a little about them. This one was part of their Aleutian line and was designed for distance and ease of handling.

"It is a sixty-five footer," Charlie proudly announced. "Like I said earlier, I got it for a great price. Her name is *Trixie's Destiny.*"

"*Trixie's Destiny*?" Scott asked, "What the hell kind of name is that, and who was Trixie? Sounds like a stripper."

Charlie chuckled. "It seems his wife was also a bit curious about the name. From what I hear, she never found out who Trixie was until he, Roger Amund, died. Turns out Trixie was a dog Roger had when he was a kid."

"He named his shiny new boat after his dog and not his wife!" Dawn laughed.

"*Trixie's Destiny*," I repeated the name, not knowing what else to say, as I tried to absorb all I was seeing and hearing.

"Charlie," Dawn said in disbelief, "you don't know the first thing about handling or maintaining a yacht like this!"

"Does it have a captain? A real captain, I mean?" Scott asked.

"Just me. There had been one back when Roger Amund owned it, but he disappeared around the time Roger died."

"Charlie…you really, truly need a captain, a skipper or whatever you want to call it, and probably a crew. You can't handle this yourself!" Dawn stressed.

"I know that!" he responded defensively. "But I don't want to have a yacht just to have someone I don't know drive me around in it. What fun would that be? I want to be the captain and drive it, damn it!"

"Holy mother of all things sane," Scott chuckled. "Charlie, my friend, you really, really, need someone to help you with this big-ass boat. You can't do it yourself!"

Charlie just looked at us while sporting another of his big goofy grins. "That's where the three of you come in."

~ ~ ~ ~ ~ ~

4: Floating Crime Scene

We stood there on the floating dock in the light drizzle, with the sound of seagulls squawking and the scent of fresh rain mixed with salty air, as we looked toward the stately yacht. It spanned almost the entire width of the t-end of the dock, far outsizing other boats near us. The yacht sported a gleaming white hull with a matching white cabin superstructure. The top deck, the fly bridge, had a hardtop cover. I could also see it held a sizeable tender to the aft. Everything about the boat was absolutely stunning. Practical, and somewhat squared off in design, but beautiful.

"At least you bought an American boat," Scott stated, seeing the name *Grand Banks* on the side of the cabin structure. Scott, we all had learned, had a real hang-up about buying American.

"Yep," Charlie responded.

"They aren't American made. This boat was made in Malaysia." I responded, dashing Scott's assessment with a bit of info I had gleaned in my earlier yacht-buying day-dreams and web searches.

"It isn't?" Scott responded aghast.

"It isn't?" Charlie added at the same time. "But the Grand Banks are in this country, right?"

"Forget where it was made, Charlie," Dawn said, putting a stop to this line of discussion. "I have just one little, bitty question, seeing how you don't even know where your boat was made: Have you even taken a ride on it?"

He looked a bit sheepish. "Nah. The water was rough the day I looked at it, so we weren't able to go out. They, the boat sales guys, said it rides nice, and I should like it and all."

The three of us just stared at our friend, absolutely stunned.

"Charlie, my friend," Scott said aghast, "I really don't know what to say other than; Holy hell, are you nuts!"

Ignoring this, Charlie stepped up to the boat, scratching his head for a moment as he looked the boat over. "When they showed it to me, we stepped through a little opening near the back port side of the boat. It's here somewhere."

"That is the starboard side, Charlie," I chuckled. I couldn't help myself. For the whole week of our group's cruise to Alaska, Charlie was frequently lost while on board and never had been confident about which side of the ship was port or which one was starboard. For me, remembering it was easy. The word "Starboard" is longer than the word "Port" and it just so happens that "Starboard" is on the right side of a boat when facing forward. Both words are the longer of the pair. Starboard vs. Port. Right vs. Left. It had made sense to me, but my little bit of logic often got blank stares when I tried to explain it.

"Well, crap!" Charlie mumbled in embarrassment.

I decided not to put Charlie down again; he seemed to be taking our jabs a bit hard. At least, I wouldn't rip on him for another two or three minutes. Charlie just gave us too many great opportunities to, well, playfully react.

I often thought of Charlie as our group's goofy genius: absolutely brilliant in some ways, and totally clueless in others. He reminded me of the character Sheldon on the TV show *Big Bang*…smart and dumb all rolled into one person.

Charlie fumbled around for a bit along the side of the boat looking for an entrance, and finally giving up. He went to the aft end where he was able to step down from the dock onto a small swim platform, and then up a set of sea stairs into the cockpit, the rear seating area of the boat.

We followed cautiously along until we were all standing in the covered back area of the boat where we were out of the wet air. Charlie fiddled in his coat pockets, perhaps looking for keys.

"You sure you own this thing?" Scott questioned, the retired cop in him coming out. "Wouldn't want to have the real owner come up with a shotgun or anything." He then nodded toward a man who was standing halfway down the dock, examining us through a pair of binoculars. "Like the guy down there."

"I am the real owner, damn it!"

Dawn, pacing around as she watched Charlie fumble for the keys, loudly complained. "I don't care who owns the freaking boat. Just let me in so I can find a bathroom-head-potty or whatever the hell you want to call it!" She glared at Charlie, "I...HAVE...TO...PEE!"

"Oh, I forgot," Charlie said apologetically as he finally found the correct key, inserting it into the lock of the sliding door from the cockpit and then opening it.

"Well, trust me, I didn't!" Dawn complained as she pushed past Charlie, darting into the interior of the boat. It was dark due to the gray skies and no lights on inside. "I know there is a john in here somewhere!" She frantically looked around.

"There isn't one on this floor," Charlie called out to her. "Go down the stairs near the front, over by the driver's seat."

I couldn't restrain myself. "On this floor?" I repeated what Charlie had said, ignoring my resolve to play nice with him for a while. "And...'by the driver's seat'?" I laughed out loud. "Charlie, you have got to be shitting me!"

"Why, what's wrong?" He sounded wounded once again.

I turned and looked at Scott who was struggling to keep from bursting out laughing. "Charlie, floors are called decks on boats."

"Oh," Charlie responded sheepishly.

"And, oh mighty Captain, the 'driver's seat'? Really? Even I know they aren't called that!"

"Then, what's it called?"

"Hell if I know. I just know there is nothing called a 'driver's seat' on a yacht. It's probably called the captain's chair, or helm, or something."

"You know, you guys can totally suck the fun out of things," Charlie responded morosely.

We entered the inviting interior of the spacious yacht. Warm wood, leather couches and teak flooring. While I tend to prefer a more light-and-airy European-style yacht, I had to admit this traditional styling was nearly perfect, although a bit dark inside. The decor totally fit the Puget Sound with its Northwest woodsy flavor. I wouldn't have picked it out for the Caribbean, but around here, in this pine tree, snow-capped mountain existence, it worked.

"Wow!" Scott whistled softly as he stepped further into the yacht while he and I looked around. "Charlie, I have to admit it. I am totally, one-hundred percent impressed."

"Me too," I added, both in sincerity, and wanting to build up Charlie's morale a bit. A person could live here in style. I reached down to examine one high-gloss wood cabinet as Charlie explained there was a large flat-panel TV hidden in it. We moved further into the yacht, heading toward the front that was partially open to view. I could see the galley was up a couple of steps, adjacent to the raised pilothouse.

Dawn came back up from the lower deck to join us. "Hey, Charlie, did you know there is blood down there in the bathroom?"

Charlie openly cringed. "Yep. That's where the murder happened."

"Murder!" the three of us exclaimed as we all turned to face him.

"What the hell, Charlie!" I added.

"Didn't I tell you?"

"You said the owner, some guy named Roger, died and his wife thought the boat was bad luck, so she sold it cheap. You said nothing about any murder," I reminded him.

"Oh," he looked downward. "That's why she wanted to get rid of it. Someone murdered her husband on this boat over in Port Townsend. Happened a few months ago. It was in the news and all."

"So, we are standing in the middle of a freaking floating crime scene?" Dawn was incredulous.

"Yep. Kinda interesting, huh?"

~ ~ ~ ~ ~ ~

TRIXIE'S DESTINY - INTERIOR LAYOUT

MAIN DECK   LOWER DECK

5: Blood Spatter

We were on a boat where a murder had occurred, seemingly, recently. Maybe to Dawn and Scott, the retired cops in the group, standing in the midst of a murder scene might seem normal. To me, a guy who had devoted the last decade of his career to conducting sales training and crafting clever Power Point presentations, this definitely wasn't an average daily occurrence.

"Show us," Scott nearly demanded. The whole event had turned from playful to deadly serious in a heartbeat. My friend Scott now seemed to stand a bit taller, his demeanor no longer that of a laid-back jokester. I was now seeing him for what he had been for decades…a professional policeman.

"It's dark down there," Dawn said. "I couldn't find a light switch. If it hadn't been for a bit of light coming through a small window, I wouldn't have seen it."

"Porthole," I corrected.

"Really?" she responded dryly, "We're talking about murder, and you're worried what I call a stupid window?"

She gave me one of those withering looks women are so good at.

I reminded myself to stop correcting the others on the terms they were using. It is a good way to lose friends.

"I didn't see it until I was done," Dawn clarified. "Probably a good thing. The point is, there wasn't much light, but there was enough for me to see blood spatter. Trust me; I know blood spatter when I see it."

I did trust her on this. As a former police detective, I knew Dawn Rollins had seen more than her share of horrible things. Enough that she had finally reached her limit and had taken an early retirement. She was the youngest of our foursome, I think. Dawn never told her age, and we didn't dare ask. I would guess she was in her late fifties...a well-preserved fifty-something who could still turn heads. The rest of us are probably a good decade older. Whatever her age, we did know that she had retired early, simply because she had told us so. We just had no clue as to how early that retirement was.

Scott looked around and found a light switch. It didn't work. No lights came on. "Charlie, dammit, how do you turn the power for this damn boat on?"

Once again, Charlie looked sheepish. More-and-more we were learning how little Charlie knew about this grand purchase of his. "I don't know. I'm sorry," he replied, again defensively.

I think we had gone a long way toward denting our new captain's ego today. "Let's go see if we can figure it out, Charlie," I prompted, leading him over to the helm where we gazed at an intimidating array of switches and gauges. Finally, off to one side, I saw a red covered switch with the simple label of, "Master."

Nudging Charlie, I pointed out the switch. I was darned if I was going to flip it on. If someone was going to blow up the boat by activating a switch, I didn't want it to be me.

The switch worked. Charlie first had to unlock it with a small key, but it worked. My guess was the master power was kept under lock so an intruder could not easily turn on and steal the expensive yacht.

With the switch turned on, a number of discretely hidden LED lights came on. It was enough to give a soft glow throughout. Glancing down the stairs to the lower deck, I could see some lights were even on down there now.

With the lights on, Scott darted down the stairs. Dawn was close behind, directing Scott to the head she had used. The door was still open. Scott flipped on an overhead light in the small room, enabling the two of them to look in and examine the scene. "Charlie," Scott called over his shoulder. "It isn't bad, but Dawn is right. There is some blood here."

"I know. I know. I should have had it cleaned before showing *Trixie* to you," he bemoaned. "It's the only place though. I looked and didn't find anywhere else onboard with blood. The police did too, or so I was told. They didn't find any more. Just this one area."

"This will need to be cleaned. By a specialist. You don't fool around with blood," Scott stated firmly.

"I actually have a clean-up crew scheduled to come in soon. Monday, I think."

With this pronouncement, we returned up the stairs and back into the pilothouse where we found an adjacent booth-like dining table on the starboard side. This was handy as the helm, dining area and galley formed a functional triangle in the raised pilothouse section of the main deck.

Scott stepped over to a door next to the booth, opening it to let the fresh, cool, salty air come in. He then joined the rest of us as we sat at the dining table booth and pondered the situation.

"One big-ass boat. One murder scene with everything in place except for the yellow crime-scene tape, a missing former captain, and one green, seasick-prone, new captain. Have I missed anything?" Dawn summarized for us.

"That about sums it up," I chuckled. "By the way, *Trixie's Destiny* is an odd name for a boat. Is that really what you want as a name for your shiny, newish, blood-stained yacht?"

"Isn't it supposed to be bad luck to change the name on a boat? Excuse me, yacht?" Scott asked.

"This boat-yacht has had its quota of bad luck already," Dawn added. "I don't think changing the name will make it any worse."

I had to laugh. A few years back I had looked this up and did learn of some sort of ritual one could do. I forget the details, only loosely remembering the general theme of the name-changing event. "I think you can change a boat's name without generating bad luck with some sort of unique ceremony. It's something like having to do a special chant while naked and dancing backward in a circle."

This got a loud laugh out of Dawn and Scott. Charlie just looked bewildered...again.

"Guys," Dawn laughed, "if you want do some sort of mojo-changing, backward-dancing, naked chant, I'll be glad to bang on a drum or something, but you can count me out of the rest of it!"

"I think I'll just keep the name. I sort of like it," Charlie said with a note of uncertainty in his voice. "You're right that I don't know much about how to steer this boat of mine, but I do know enough to get a bit of training. I've hired someone to come up here next week from Seattle who will provide some hands-on training."

"You'll need it," Scott stated.

"We all need it. Plus, I learned the insurance company won't insure my yacht until I—we—have completed the training," Charlie added. "I want you all to join me. I need my co-captains."

"Don't you need some sort of license to pilot a boat like this?" Dawn asked.

I knew the answer but was curious to see if Charlie did as well. I was pleased to see he did.

"Oddly, no. You need a license if you are going to get paid for the work, but not if you are going to just drive your own boat. Kinda interesting. Like I said, I need training to keep the insurance company off my back."

"You need training just so you won't bump into stuff with this big boat!" Scott added derisively.

"We will all learn how to not 'bump into stuff', as you put it," Charlie responded simply. "If you are in with me, that is. I want to take long trips in it, maybe even up to Alaska, and I need you with me."

It didn't take me more than a moment to think about it. I was in. Right after I retired, my wife, Francine, and I had done the usual new-retiree thing of traveling to far-flung places, and then we had sold our house in Ohio and moved out here to be closer to our daughter, Emily, where we now had a "lifestyle home" with a view toward Fidalgo Bay. With little more to do now, other than stare out at the view, I was bored stiff. Yes, I was in on Charlie's new venture. I would be one of his co-captains.

"Count me in," I told Charlie and the others.

B G Preston

"Oh, what the hell," Dawn added. "The worst we can do is drown."

"Or get captured by pirates," Scott added.

"There are no pirates in the Puget Sound," Charlie added confidently.

"Tell that to the first guy who comes up to this shiny boat of yours with a gun in hand," Scott responded stiffly. "Oh, what the hell, I'm in too. Or, I will be once I clear it with the missus." He was referring to his wife, Sally. Despite Scott's career in law enforcement, Sally was clearly the ruler of the family.

Charlie like to tell Scott that his wife had him by the balls and wasn't about to let go. Whenever Charlie said this, Scott could only cringe at the unfortunate truth.

I had no doubt that an interesting, and heated, discussion between the two was likely to ensue.

"So, we're all in?" Charlie asked, hopefully. "We're all about to be the proud crew of *Trixie's Destiny*!"

~ ~ ~ ~ ~ ~

6: Who Sleeps Where?

We were about to be inducted into the *Trixie's Destiny* crew. Great, but scary in a way. I had often fantasized of owning a yacht, now it seemed I was going to have much of the privilege, but without having to lay out the large chunk of cash to do so. All I would have to do was to come on board from time-to-time, have some fun acting as part of the crew, and leave all of the hassle and expense to Charlie.

Now, I liked Charlie more than ever.

We explored the rest of the multi-deck yacht and Charlie's impromptu tour was to start with the top deck, the fly bridge. From the pilothouse, Charlie prepared to lead us up a wooden stairway to the fly bridge above. He only made it a few steps before he came to an abrupt halt. A hatchway covered the top of the stairway and it was clear that Charlie didn't know what to do. If there was a latch to open it, he wasn't finding it as we watched him fumble about while standing a couple feet higher than us.

Another opportunity to rip on Charlie, but I held back. I had put in my quota for one day.

Scott, the impatient one of the group, grew tired of looking up at Charlie's butt as he was several steps above us, fiddling with a latch. He left us and disappeared without saying anything. I hadn't really tried to follow his actions as my attention was on Charlie. Soon, to our surprise, the hatchway was pulled open from above, and there stood a smiling Scott, looking down at us. "It was latched from up here," he said simply, obviously proud of himself. "I used that key of yours, which you left on the table, to open it."

"Oh," Charlie responded in a low voice, perhaps embarrassed at Scott's figuring it out before he did.

Within moments, we all had found our way up the steep stairs and onto the covered fly bridge. This was the place to be. The high, open perch gave a wonderful view in all directions. We could easily see the bow ahead of us with the marina and jetty in the distance. A number of comfortable seats were positioned near the helm, giving everyone up there a great view, along with being covered by the hard top which spanned most of the fly bridge. This, I knew, was where I was likely to spend as much time as possible when onboard.

We explored the fly bridge and examined the controls, while acting as if we knew what we were looking at, and then explored the rear—aft—section of the upper deck. There, we saw a large tender with a motor on it. Next to the tender was some sort of crane. I assumed it was to facilitate moving the tender down into and out of the water.

While standing next to the tarp-covered tender, Scott nudged me, causing me to look back down the floating dock. The man who had been staring at us from halfway down the marina was at it again. This time he appeared to be taking pictures. "What do you think he's up to?" Scott said to no one in particular.

"Probably just admiring this boat and wishing he were on it with us," I said simply. Somehow, I didn't think this was quite true. There was something about the look of the guy I didn't like. Apparently, Scott didn't either.

"So, we give him what he is giving us," Dawn said. She stood against the railing and made an obvious show of taking pictures of the guy with her cellphone. That did it. The man quickly turned and went back to the marina entrance, keeping his back to us the whole time.

"Back to our tour," I said. "Charlie, show us more. If we are going to be co-captains, I would like to know more about what I will be co-captaining."

Charlie was happy to take me up on the offer. Explorations of the fly bridge done, we went back down the forward stairs, into the pilothouse, and then down another set of stairs to the lower deck. Charlie joyfully led us into an interior, now lit, short hall where we found three cabins, each with its own head. One of the cabins was huge. The other two were of good size. They were nothing close to the size of a cabin on a cruise ship, but there was plenty of room to sleep in comfort.

"Hey, there are three bedrooms and there are four of us. I assume, Charlie, that since this big-ass boat is yours, you get that large bedroom, and the rest of us get the smaller rooms," Dawn stated. "So, who is going to share a room? Oh, I definitely get my own bedroom!"

"Cabin," I clarified with a broad smile. So much for my resolve to stop correcting the terms the others were using.

She just glared. A playful glare, but wow, could she drill into you with those eyes. I can only imagine what the bad guys must have thought back when she was working as a detective and conducting interrogations. "One more, Frank, and I'm tossing your retired corporate-guy butt overboard."

"Can I watch?" Scott joined in.

"I think there is another place to sleep," Charlie said, scratching his head as he looked about.

"What, on a pull-out couch somewhere?" Scott complained.

"I seem to remember seeing another sleeping area when they showed me the boat," Charlie mulled aloud.

He wandered up and down the small, wood-paneled passageway, as if looking for a door to a hidden cabin. Suddenly his face lit up. Without saying anything, he darted up the stairway and back to the pilothouse. We had no choice except to do likewise. We continued to follow him through the salon and out to the covered aft section. Charlie paused again as we just stood nearby watching him try to figure it out.

"Looks like you've run out of ideas," Scott prodded our friend.

"There's another door around here somewhere. I remember! There is a little door on the starboard side!" Charlie exclaimed proudly as he led us to the port side of the boat and a few feet forward. Oh, I wanted to say something about the port vs. starboard thing again but didn't dare.

Soon, he found a small door and he led us down a very steep set of wooden stairs into the lower deck again. It seemed this sizeable, porthole-free area didn't connect up with the cabin area up forward, even though they were all on the same deck. We looked around, seeing two narrow bunks along the walkway and a small head. This, I quickly realized, was the crew area.

"This is mine!" Dawn exclaimed. "It can be my own private little oasis away from you three."

If she wanted this dark and confined area for herself, fine. I wasn't about to argue.

Our last bit of exploration was to step into the engine room that had a connecting door to the crew area. I am not a mechanic, and never will be, so all I could do when looking at this room was to stand in awe. Before us, in an impressively large room, stood two huge diesel engines, plus more pieces of complex equipment than I could count.

Scott laughed out loud at seeing this. He knew Charlie was absolutely helpless around machinery. Pretty much like the rest of us. "And, you're sure you don't need to hire a crew? A real crew...folks who know what to do with all of this stuff?"

For the first time, Charlie looked uncertain. I don't think he had even seen the engine room of his expensive yacht before. Now, as he stood looking around him at the incredible array of machinery and equipment, I could see him going white. "We'll figure it out. I hope."

With that, we knew we definitely had some interesting times ahead.

~ ~ ~ ~ ~ ~

7: Francine

The chat with my wife, Francine, that evening was a bit rocky at first.

I had played out my little speech in my mind several times and it had sounded fine to me. When it came time to actually tell her about Charlie, *Trixie's Destiny*, and our plans, I mucked it up.

"I know I said you needed to get a hobby or something to keep you busy, but this?" she had responded while shaking her head. "Have you ever even been on a boat like that before?" she asked, and then quickly answered for me...a habit of hers. "No. You haven't! And, now you want to be a member of Charlie's crew. Have you completely lost it?"

Wow, harsh. "Co-captain, not crew. I am a co-captain." That, honestly, was the best I could come up with. It was totally lame, and she knew it.

She didn't have the glare down like Dawn did. Her method was to put reality in your face. I hated that. Reality can suck. I like the not-having-thought-it-through-at-all approach much better than cold reality. "We'll be okay. We're getting training." Another lame response on my part.

"Does Charlie know anything about boating?" She asked the one question I was most afraid of.

"He knows some stuff." My third incredibly poor response. I was not winning this one.

"Oh, well, stuff. Then, who could ask for more."

Despite her shock and reservations at this proposed venture, she eventually came around to agreeing to it in a you-are-nuts kind of way. It just took a while to get there.

I think she would have preferred that I take up stamp collecting.

Francine mostly wanted to make sure that I was going into this with my eyes wide open and I wouldn't die in the process. She did have some very real concerns and suggestions for what we should do, but she didn't really try to stop me. I didn't even sense her usual passive resistance to it.

She knew how bored I was. Francine also knew how I had often fantasized about owning a boat, something she had no desire to do. I had dragged her through a boat show once, years ago back in Ohio, but she had zero appreciation of the boats and equipment on display. We left the exhibition early, resulting in complete obliteration of my boat-buying fantasy.

Now, an incredible opportunity had shown up, and I wanted to do it, but I didn't want to cause a serious rift in the relationship with my wife in the process.

We talked the plan through for a while and I answered what few questions I could. It helped that I was able to report how this particular brand and model had an excellent safety record. Although, putting four know-nothing people in command didn't exactly make for a safe situation. I tried to focus the discussion on the safety aspects of the boat, and not on Charlie, Scott, Dawn and me.

After a while, we both saw this was going to work out perfectly. Perfectly, that is, if I didn't get killed in the process. It would give her more free time to spend with our granddaughter and be able to do so without feeling like she had to keep me company every moment of the day. Our daughter, Emily, had a two-year old, Emma, and my wife was totally enjoying her newfound role as babysitter to Emma.

The one big concern Francine had was with Dawn. It was one thing to have a woman as part of our Thursday morning coffee chat. It was a horse of another color for me to potentially spend days at a time, and nights, on a yacht with her. It also didn't help that Dawn was an attractive woman. The one mitigating factor here was that my wife knew her and knew how she was unlikely to ever try to get it on with a married guy.

Dawn's husband had messed around on her and it had stung badly. It was clear to us all that Dawn was not going to be "the other woman" in any relationship. She knew the harm it could cause.

"Just, well, just don't even think about it," my wife said simply.

I could only agree. My focus was on boating, not on other activities.

Still… men-will be-boys when it comes to women.

So, other than not having a clue about how to navigate, handle, manage, fix, dock, or anything on a yacht, I was primed and ready. I couldn't wait for our training to begin.

~ ~ ~ ~ ~ ~

8: Captain Rick

I used to love the old movie *Captain Ron*, starring Kurt Russell as a highly questionable yacht captain. The movie took place on an old charter sailboat in the Caribbean, and Captain Ron was as crusty an individual as you would ever want to encounter.

Our trainer, Captain Rick, was the spitting image of how I might have imagined Captain Ron to be at the age of fifty. His uniform, if you could call it that, had likely never seen a washing machine, let alone an iron. His paunch betrayed his love of beer, and the good captain's hair was almost as wild and crazy as the look in his eyes.

All that was missing was the eyepatch like Kurt Russel had worn in the movie. Funny thing, in that movie, Kurt Russell's eyepatch kept switching from one eye to another.

"Where the hell did you come up with this guy?" Scott said anxiously to Charlie as we stood on the dock alongside *Trixie's Destiny*, watching our soon-to-be trainer, Captain Rick, amble up the dock toward us.

"I found him in the yellow pages," Charlie said with a straight face.

"Charlie, no one uses the yellow pages anymore! Did you ever think of looking online? You know, you could turn on that computer you have and never use. You can actually find out stuff on it—like reviews—so you could learn if this guy is worth a crap!" Scott berated Charlie.

"I'm not stupid!" Charlie retorted.

I could tell he was also disconcerted about how Captain Rick looked but was probably too embarrassed to admit it.

As I watched Captain Rick work his way toward us, it seemed he could barely walk a straight line. I hoped he would do better on the water.

Captain Rick wasn't the only one with a questionable appearance. At Charlie's insistence, we were all wearing our shiny new captain and co-captain's caps. Charlie had also purchased new navy blue windbreakers so we would look like we belonged together as a crew. This would have been fine except for the six-inch high letters, *Trixie's Destiny*, emblazoned in bright yellow on the back of each of the windbreakers. Our names were on the front of each jacket, in equally bright lettering.

We looked absolutely stupid. Did Charlie really think we would wear these anywhere in public?

It seems he did.

"Oh, my lord!" Captain Rick exclaimed as he came closer, stopping to look us over. He then broke out into a fit of laughter.

"Is there something wrong?" Charlie asked, obviously offended.

Captain Rick looked around, scratched his head a moment, and laughed again. "You guys are what real yachters joke about in every marina across this planet!"

This guy was ticking me off. Yes, we're totally green, but hell, this is why Charlie had hired him.

Without so much as a basic "good morning" or introduction of any sort, he proceeded to grill us one-by-one to learn more of our skill level. I could have told him in one easy word…zero.

Charlie proudly announced that he had read a few chapters in a book on boating.

"*Boating for Dummies?*" Captain Rick asked, scorn oozing from him.

Again, this guy was pissing me off, but then I caught the embarrassed look on Charlie's face. Holy hell! Charlie actually had been reading *Boating for Dummies*.

"Maybe," Charlie admitted.

I could have died from embarrassment but didn't have the chance as it was my turn to be grilled by Captain Rick. I couldn't even say I had read any of *Boating for Dummies*.

Did taking a cruise and walking through a boat show count as experience?

Captain Rick, having learned that our collective experience was, well, nothing, just shook his head again. He then stepped to the side while visually assessing *Trixie's Destiny*. "You will destroy that beautiful boat inside of ten minutes. Sell it now, or hire somebody with experience, I beg you!"

"We want to be trained. This is my yacht, and I want for all four of us to be given some professional training," Charlie said, affronted.

"Let me guess," Captain Rick responded sarcastically. "Your insurance company is making you do this, right?"

"Well," Charlie confessed, "that too."

Captain Rick snickered, reached into an old blue canvas satchel he was carrying and pulled out something. Brochures. He handed one to each of us, turned, and walked away as he shook his head in dismay.

"Hey, where are you going?" Charlie called out to him.

"You get some basic classroom training and some experience, and then maybe we will talk. Oh, and take off those stupid caps!"

"But I paid you already!" Charlie yelled out as the crusty captain wandered further down the dock.

"Thanks, I appreciate it," Captain Rick responded as he gave a back-of-the-hand wave to us.

It would seem our training was at an end.

"That was rude!" I exclaimed. "What a jerk. If he doesn't like to train novices, then why did he make the drive all the way up here from Seattle?"

"Charlie?" Dawn asked, drawing his name out into multiple syllables. "Exactly what did you say to that guy when you hired him?"

Charlie looked sheepish as he looked down to his feet while answering. "I might have overstated our experience a bit. He did say something about advanced navigation and stuff like that."

"Now, why aren't I surprised?" Scott laughed.

"What say we head over to McDuck's Coffee Bar," Dawn offered, looking down at the paper in her hand. Captain Rick had given us each a brochure from an outfit in Everett that offered boat safety and navigation courses.

"Sold," I responded. "I've had enough training for one day anyway."

We hadn't even stepped aboard *Trixie*, and the first day of our great adventure was at an end.

~ ~ ~ ~ ~ ~

9: Training

"To receive your certificate of completion, you will be tested at the end of training," Ralph Sawyer, our trainer, announced as he stood in the front of the room facing us.

"Test!" Scott exclaimed. "You have got to be kidding me!"

"Play nice," Dawn hushed our testy friend while we sat there.

"I am playing nice. I got up at the crack of dawn to drive down here with the rest of you guys, didn't I?"

"And complained all the way," I added. That morning, we had indeed gotten up way early. Together in Scott's oversized SUV, we had taken the nearly one hour drive to our training site at a facility adjacent to the Port of Everett Marina. We would have had to wait several weeks for training to be available in Anacortes, while classes were far more frequent here, thus the drive.

So, there we sat, along with six other people who had signed up for the same three-day intensive course on boating safety, navigation and seamanship. The embarrassing part was that we were, by far, the oldest ones there. Two of the other students were twin boys, about twelve years old, who had come with their father, Tony Drew.

"If those little brats do better than me on the test, I quit!" Scott complained in a harsh whisper. He was sitting at a two-person table with me and, I soon learned, had the habit of wanting to express every woe or complaint by leaning into me so he could whisper loudly in my ear.

"Personal space, fella!" I tried to ward him off. It didn't work. It seems that Scott and the concept of personal space didn't see eye-to-eye.

Training began. I had hoped we would be on a boat and we would actually learn how to, well, start and run Charlie's newish Grand Banks. It wasn't to be.

The first day was solely in a classroom. I hadn't sat in a classroom environment in years and having to do it now rather intimidated me. If Ralph Sawyer just hadn't said something about a test, I would have been okay. He had, though, so that was foremost in my worries. I'd be damned if I would fail it, and then have to go crawling back to my wife with the woeful news.

Wow was there a lot to learn! Boating regulations. Navigation. Use of marine radio. Safety, even some CPR training. Who has right of way on the water. Basic boat maintenance. Customs regulations. And, so on it went.

We four were totally numb by the end of the day.

Luckily, we had opted to stay in a hotel at the marina instead of driving back home. It was only an hour drive, but we really didn't have it in us to drive back to Anacortes. That little hotel was just fine.

"Those damn kids," Scott complained yet again while we guzzled a beer over a dinner of fish and chips. "This isn't right!"

"What isn't right, Scott?" Dawn asked, but I could see she was just leading him on.

"It! It isn't right!" Scott complained loudly.

"Oh. 'It'. Of course," Dawn laughed. If she had any reservations about going through training alongside young kids, it didn't show. For some reason that Scott never made clear, he was really bugged by it.

And, that was it for the first day. Just lots and lots of stuff thrown at us, followed by lots of stuff to study and remember.

That night in my hotel room, feeling totally stressed, I read and reread through the day's training material. Somehow, I finally dozed off, but I can't say it was the best night's sleep I'd ever had.

On the second day, we actually got onto a boat. It wasn't much of one, but enough for our instructor to teach us the basic tricks of maneuvering a boat, tying it to a dock, the parts of a boat and using lines and fenders. Fenders are like big rubber bumpers you place between the boat and the dock to keep the boat from getting damaged.

I was worried. We were being taught on a boat about twenty-five feet long. Would any of this knowledge even apply when we tried to manage Charlie's big-ass sixty-five footer?

According to Ralph, yes.

I had pulled him aside and expressed my worries. After he realized we were adamant that it would be us, and not a professional captain, in command of *Trixie's Destiny*, he relented and said that, in some ways, it would be even easier. A yacht like Charlie's would have thrusters, a joystick control and other gizmos on the boat, making maneuvering less tricky.

His two cautions were to always go very, very slow when in a marina because we were pushing a heavy boat around, and to always have at least two people on board. A small boat, like our training boat, could be easily managed by one. *Trixie's Destiny* would need two or more: one person to maneuver it, someone else to manage the fenders, tying it to the dock and keeping a watch out for problems.

On-the-water training included docking maneuvers. I was happy to see this, the concept of backing up that large yacht into a narrow slip scared the heck out of me.

So, we did those docking maneuvers over and over. It seems that my previous fears were well-founded. Charlie, Scott and I were horrible! Dawn seemed to be just fine, but I paid little attention. It was my lack of boat-handling skill that was primary among my embarrassment and worries.

Those two twelve-year-old kids were perfect. I mean, they slid our training boat into the slip like it was nothing. It didn't matter if they were docking nose in or backing the boat in to the slip. They were perfect every time.

I hated those kids just then.

I also think I owe the training school for the cost of re-painting one side of their little training boat. My attempt at docking would have been comical if it hadn't been quite so pathetic and, well, damaging.

None of us drank anything after our second day of training. We were to take the test the next day, and the foreknowledge of that test put us all on edge. Who'd a thunk that a little boating safety test would freak us all out so much?

"Want to place a bet on who gets the best score?" Dawn jested.

She didn't get any takers on the bet.

~ ~ ~ ~ ~ ~

10: Intruder

Our test results arrived via email the next day, along with an attached certificate of completion and instructions to print it out and keep it with us.

"Pass-fail!" Scott moaned.

"Had he told us that earlier, I wouldn't have been so stressed out!" I whined as I sipped my half-finished Duzy-sized coffee while eyeing the last McBeignet which sat in the cheap plastic basket. One more second and it would have been mine. Scott beat me to it.

Actually, I was fine with the pass-fail thing; it put us all at the same accomplishment level. Had one of us earned a much lower score than the others, there is no telling how many verbal jabs that person would have had to endure.

Unless, of course, I had received the highest score and then I would have been the one to dish out the punishment to the others. That might have been fun. Now, we would never know.

We were back in McDuck's Coffee Bar on the morning following our training, waiting for Charlie to join us. He was late—an unusual thing for him. Our goal for the day was to go back on board *Trixie,* actually start it up and then, hopefully, even take her out. I think this scared us all more than a little.

Charlie had called Captain Rick to see if he would now deign to work with us. Even with our training completed, it still seemed like a good idea to have someone like Captain Rick with us. But it wasn't to be. The crusty captain was fully booked.

Maybe that yellow pages ad was working, after all.

"I just hope one of those brat kids failed it," Scott complained as we went on to discuss our test results.

We still didn't know why Scott was so hung up about it.

"That's horrible!" Dawn said. "Those kids were nice and very well behaved."

"That's just the problem. I've been a cop too long. I don't trust 'nice.' Evil I get, not nice!"

"They were all nice, and I think it's great that we all passed and got our certificates. I just wish we knew our exact scores. Then I could see who won the bet," Dawn added.

"Uh, none of us ever took you up on that bet," I reminded her.

"Did too!"

I didn't dare counter her. I had learned from many years of marriage to never tell a woman she didn't remember something correctly. It was a losing proposition.

"Hey, you only think those kids were nice because you had a thing for their dad. Tony, something or other. You made goo-goo eyes at him more than once that I could see and there was definite flirting going on," Scott lightheartedly added.

I would never have been that brave. If Dawn had ever made "goo-goo eyes" at anyone, I certainly had not seen that side of her, nor would I have announced it as Scott just had.

"Hey, Anthony, uh, Tony, is a widower, almost my age, and, well, just zip it!"

Holy cow, she was actually embarrassed!

"Guys! Problem!" We all heard Mac anxiously call out to us from behind the counter. He was pointing out the window to a spot in the parking lot about halfway between us and the marina entrance.

It was Charlie. A face dripping with blood, Charlie. He was hobbling our way.

"What the hell!" Scott exclaimed as he, and then Dawn, quickly exited our booth and darted out the door. I followed close behind.

Scott was first to arrive, putting an arm around Charlie, and guiding him to lean against a car there in the parking lot so that Scott could look him over.

Again, with a likely emergency at hand, the professional side of Scott had come out and impressed me. The 'retired-guy' version of Scott was laid back and a bit of a jokester. This other, rarely-seen side of him was impressive and totally different.

"An intruder! Someone broke into *Trixie*!" Charlie exclaimed. "I had gone on board to make sure that the cleaning crew had done their work while we were in Everett and he was there."

"Don't say anything else," Dawn commanded as she looked into Charlie's eyes as to check out his wounded forehead. "I think you will be okay, but let's get you looked at by a doctor just in case."

Hearing this, Scott pulled out his cellphone and was soon commanding instructions to the 911 dispatcher, informing them in precise detail what was going on and what was needed.

Scott and Dawn were definitely two people you wanted to have around you when something went wrong.

"Frank," Scott instructed me. "You stay with Charlie. Go with him and the EMS team to the hospital. Dawn will go with me to check things out at the boat."

I had wanted to go with Scott to check out the boat and was a bit disappointed, but it made sense that the two retired officers would be the ones to do so. I just wish I could have been there to watch them in action.

Crafting sales presentations, back in my career in marketing, had never been this interesting. Except maybe for the time I misspelled the name of the company president when making a presentation to the entire sales force. Now that was an interesting moment.

During Scott's 911 call, he had also requested the local police, and they were to be there before anyone went on board *Trixie*. There was no doubt in my mind that Scott and Dawn would be leading the pack.

~ ~ ~ ~ ~ ~

11: The Adventure Grows

Luckily, everything was okay. Charlie had little more than a head scratch and a minor bump.

His pride was wounded more than his head. That and the fact that the event had scared the crap out of him.

Scott and Dawn met up with us at the emergency room just as Charlie was being released. The doctor had looked him over, declaring Charlie fit, but cautioned him to rest a bit.

"How is *Trixie*?" Charlie asked, his worry showing in his face.

"A little bit of a mess, but nothing serious," Scott succinctly replied. "He must have had a key; there is no sign of forced entry. Some stuff was littered about, and we put most everything back in place."

"Enough about the yacht," Dawn interjected. "Charlie, tell us what happened when you boarded the yacht. Did you see the guy? Assuming it was a man that hit you."

Charlie wasn't able to provide a lot of help. He had boarded *Trixie's Destiny*, noticed the opened side door and stepped in. He had gone in just a few feet when he heard a noise, turned toward it, and that was when someone had whacked his head.

"I couldn't find what they might have hit you with. Luckily, it couldn't have been anything substantial. Otherwise you would have had a much bigger injury," Scott clarified.

"Charlie, it was clear that the intruder, or intruders, were looking for something. Also, given the focused nature of the clutter, it seems that they were looking for something specific. Any ideas?" Dawn asked.

"None. None at all," he said woefully.

"Could they have had a key? To me, it seems like someone just opened the starboard side door and let themselves in." Scott grilled Charlie.

"No one else has a key that I know of. Oh, except for the marina and cleaning people who are supposed to watch over the boat and maintain it, oh, and I heard from my dead cousin's wife that the former captain showed up asking about the yacht, and he probably has a key, and I think the company who sold me the boat may still have a key, oh, and…"

"Holy crap!" Scott exclaimed, interrupting Charlie. "Maybe I should have asked who doesn't have a key. The list would have been shorter."

"Okay, Captain Charlie, just what the hell have you gotten us all into?" Dawn asked.

"I don't know."

"They were looking for something. My guess is it had something to do with the former owner, Roger Amund. Do you have any idea what he was up to?" Dawn was in full interrogation mode now.

"I barely knew him. I do know that he got his money from some sort of import-export business," Charlie explained lamely.

Dawn and Scott laughed simultaneously.

"What? What's so funny?"

Scott just shook his head. "Charlie, you don't have to be a retired cop to see the issue here. Don't you ever watch any spy movies or murder mysteries?"

Charlie simply nodded in affirmation.

Dawn, chuckling, continued. "Captain Charlie, the overused stereotype in every one of those movies is that anyone involved in import-export is a bad guy. You know; drugs, stolen goods, money laundering, or who knows what. The point is, as much as it pains me to say it, things seem to be pointing toward that stereotype."

"Uh, oh," Charlie muttered.

"Things like a missing captain who mysteriously reappears. Your cousin getting killed. Someone watching our every move the first day we explored *Trixie*, and now someone is breaking into her!" Scott summarized.

"Well, crap. So, what do we do?"

"Do you still want to keep your yacht and take trips on her?" Dawn grilled Charlie.

"Yes! I want to cruise to places and stuff."

"Stuff," Dawn chuckled in response. "Well, if you want to do stuff with your boat then we do exactly what we were planning on doing. Have a lot of fun by taking trips on *Trixie's Destiny*. We just keep a watch out," Dawn clarified.

"And we keep our weapons with us on the boat!" Scott added.

"Really?" Charlie asked, surprised, "Is that necessary?"

"Yep. Otherwise, you can count me out."

"He's right, Charlie," Dawn confirmed. "Something's amiss with this boat and we don't want to find out what it is the hard way."

"This adventure just got way more, well, adventurous!" I stated aloud as I imagined a likely chat with my wife…"What dear, weapons? Nah, those are just odd-looking fishing rods. Why would we ever need weapons out on a yacht in the serene Puget Sound?"

Yes, it has!" Scott responded almost gleefully. "Way more adventurous!"

~ ~ ~ ~ ~ ~

12: Starting Her Up

"I think it's this switch," Charlie said nervously, looking at the array of equipment before him while sitting in the helm seat. Our good captain was about to turn on his yacht for the first time on the day following the break in to the yacht. His face had nearly gone white at the prospect of kicking the engines in gear. "I've been studying the manuals and I think I have it down."

"You're not doing a hell of a lot to build my confidence, Captain," Dawn said as we all stood there in the pilothouse, looking over Charlie's shoulder.

"It's in neutral, right?" Scott asked nervously.

"How the hell would I know?" Charlie responded defensively, his frustration was starting to show.

"So much for having studied the manual," I laughed.

I looked down at the throttles, a combination of two paired traditional handles, and I could see they were in neutral. Next to these was a small joystick. This joystick, if Charlie knew anything at all, is what he would use to actually maneuver this large yacht, at least in tight areas.

Charlie turned the switch and suddenly we could feel the gentle vibration of the engines. We had all seen the engines down below and they were huge. You would never know that though. The sound and vibration in the pilothouse were minimal.

"Hooray!" Scott exclaimed. "Nothing exploded."

I felt the same. As silly as it seemed, just the task of turning on the engines was a major accomplishment. If we could figure out how to do that, who knows, we might even figure out how to make the boat move.

As the engines continued to hum, we could see an amazing array of gauges had come to life: gauges for engine performance, navigation, fuel and water levels, radio communication, and much more.

No red lights were flashing. I took that as a positive sign.

"Do we have gas?" Dawn asked.

I glanced over Charlie's shoulder and down at the instrument panel. The fuel gauge indicated that we had more than one-thousand gallons on board. Since learning of Charlie's acquisition of *Trixie's Destiny*, I had gone online and studied what few specs I could find on the Grand Banks website. Fuel quantities was one of those, so I knew one-thousand gallons was about a half tank. More than enough to go anywhere locally but not enough for a long trip, but that didn't matter at this stage.

Another good thing about having so much fuel on board was that we wouldn't have to find our way to the fuel station for a while yet. The thought of maneuvering this boat into that busy area was daunting, even though I would not likely be the one to do it.

I just didn't want to be onboard when we crashed into the marina's gas station.

Fuel station. I inwardly laughed at the thought. The very notion of having to pay for a couple thousand gallons of diesel fuel for a single fill-up would have been enough right there to keep me from ever owning a yacht like this. No normal person could afford it.

"Let's go somewhere!" Scott declared.

Charlie, hearing this, looked nervously at each of us as we each nodded in wary confirmation.

"Wait!" I called out in a panic, as a fresh thought hit. "We're still tied up to the dock!"

"Oh," Charlie said simply. He, of all people on board, should have been the first to think of this. It made me wonder what else was not on Charlie's radar. How so much intelligence and lack of common sense could be wrapped up into one person amazed me.

Scott and I darted out of the pilothouse, over to the aft cockpit and then down onto the dock. The boat was secured with lines fore and aft. Scott released the front line from the dock. He let the line, which came from the front starboard quarter of the boat, drop into the water so that it could be pulled in later.

Once Scott was done and safely back on board, I undid the aft line, letting it drop into the water as well, then I darted on board.

Scott went forward to pull up and stow away the line while I remained in the cockpit to pull in the aft line.

I heard Scott call out to Charlie that the lines were okay, and we were good to go.

Then I was in the water!

The water in the Puget Sound is damn cold!

It seems that Captain Charlie didn't have a clue about how much power to give to the engines so, well, he way overdid it. That unexpected punch to the engines had caught me just as I was leaning over to retrieve the line, throwing me overboard in the process.

To anyone watching, it was probably a hilarious sight. To me, not so much.

Looking around from my watery position, I realized I was only a few feet from the dock, and I could see other boat owners rushing up to help me.

I didn't know if I should be pissed or embarrassed. Pissed. It wasn't my damn fault.

Soon, fully dripping from my unexpected drenching in the cold marina waters, I stood there on the dock as I watched *Trixie's Destiny* bobble to a stop about fifty or sixty yards from us, sending a confused wake around her and causing more than one boater to yell out in anger.

Our first few minutes—make that moments—at sea were not an auspicious beginning.

~ ~ ~ ~ ~ ~

13: Docking Trixie

A crowd of amused boat owners was growing as I watched the inept maneuvering of *Trixie's Destiny* from the dock. She was now about eighty yards out and drifting toward the protective rock jetty.

Even from this distance, I would swear I could hear Scott and Charlie yelling at each other. They probably were.

Slowly, with one poorly done turn after another, the large yacht was finally headed back my way. Two smaller yachts had to dart aside as Charlie cut across their right-of-way.

Another set of angry yells. Charlie's popularity wasn't exactly growing. I expected that the harbormaster would show up any minute, and I would be glad that I wasn't on *Trixie* just then.

"Any bets that that clown smashes into the dock?" one middle-aged bystander asked the crowd of about twenty.

"Five bucks that he mangles it!" another person responded.

Soon other bets were being bandied about. A few were in Charlie's favor. Most were not. I put in my five with the guy who voted that Charlie would mangle it.

I didn't have a clue as to what was going on in that pilothouse. My guess was that Charlie and Scott were arguing in half-panic while Dawn would be trying to calm them. It wouldn't be the first time that she had to settle one or more of us down. She was good at diffusing tense situations like this.

I hadn't counted on Dawn totally taking over. At some point, perhaps after the poor set of turns, the boat appeared to operate smoothly, and the signs of jerkiness were gone. I saw Scott come out to the port side, which was now facing the dock, and just stare at nothing in particular, his face a mask of anger.

The boat then turned gracefully, as if on a turntable. It was a delight to watch *Trixie's Destiny* do a full 180-degree turn. Soon, the starboard side was facing me, and both Scott and Charlie were now out on the side deck. Yes, Dawn was definitely handling the yacht.

Inch-by-inch, taking extreme care, Dawn used the thrusters to nudge the large boat over and into position. Soon, the fenders, which were still hanging over the starboard side, gently kissed the floating concrete dock.

God bless, Dawn. She had saved the day.

The bystanders cheered while some of them took the lines which Charlie and Scott were tossing out. Soon, the boat was safe and secure against the dock.

"Sorry, Frank!" Charlie called out to me.

I decided to not let my anger out. This had been hard enough on Charlie as it was.

"Ready to get back on board so we can give it another try?"

"Please, Frank," I heard Dawn, who had come out of the pilothouse and was leaning over the railing to talk to me, ignoring the small crowd of onlookers around us.

"I'm all wet."

"Go home and change. We'll wait," Dawn announced for the others.

I did exactly that. Slogging back down the long dock in my wet clothes and squeaky boat shoes, I headed for my car and then home to change.

An hour later, I was back on board. It didn't take long to go home and switch out my clothes. Luckily, Francine wasn't at home. She was at a park with our granddaughter.

Not having to explain the whole misbegotten venture to her was a blessing. It shouldn't matter, but it did. Another imagined chat with my wife..."Why am I all wet, you ask? Oh, I don't know. It's a nice day and I thought I'd just go for a swim with all of my clothes on. Oh, and sorry about ruining those shoes I just bought last week." Sure, that would go over well.

"How about if Dawn pilots us out," I suggested to the others when I returned. Scott and Dawn readily agreed. Charlie, understandably, was not happy.

"You'll have plenty of opportunity once we get out of this marina," I explained.

"Okay, but only until then. Then I take command."

I could only shudder at those words.

~ ~ ~ ~ ~ ~

14: Finally, Some Success

Dawn's ability to manipulate *Trixie* was almost perfect, much to Charlie's chagrin.

With nearly a dozen people watching us from the docks, several with cellphone cameras in hand, Scott and I again untied the lines to free the yacht from the dock, crossed our fingers as we got back onboard, and then Dawn went through her own made-up-on-the-spot checklist. It reminded me of when I took a few flying lessons way back when. There are checklists for everything in flying: pre-flight, engine start, taxiing, taking off, and a whole lot more.

Why hadn't we thought of using checklists for operating *Trixie's Destiny* before? It took Dawn's calm approach and her organizational skills to come up with this. Actually, for all any of us knew, there might be a full array of Grand Banks-provided checklists lying around somewhere. We just hadn't found them. We hadn't thought to look for them either, at least not until Dawn had made her own.

This time, no one would get dumped in the water. At least with Dawn at the helm, no one would get dumped. I wasn't so sure what would happen when Charlie, Scott or even I took the helm.

The other big difference was that we were now working from the fly bridge helm station instead of the lower pilothouse. Like I said before, I like it up here. The only issue now was all of those folks on the marina who were taking pictures of us, hoping for us to screw up again.

With so many people watching and taking pictures, we stood there on the upper bridge and acted as if we knew what the hell we were doing. We watched as Dawn used the joystick to activate the thrusters and then gently edge away from the dock. I could see more than one person on the dock put their camera away. Seeing the smooth pull out from the dock, it now seemed apparent that we weren't going to bump into anything.

"I think we disappointed some of them," I said as I waved to the crowd who were slowly fading from view.

"Let's keep it that way, fellas," Dawn said, her attention firmly on the waterway ahead. Now that we were safely away from the dock, we were depending on her to get us out of the busy marina. This meant she had to maneuver around a mix of other boats. Some had the right-of-way; some were to give way to us.

"When we are done here," Charlie said anxiously, "remind me to go and puke."

I wasn't sure if he was saying this because of the incredible stress or if he was seasick already. I certainly knew that the stress was getting to me. The puking thing that Charlie had mentioned was sounding pretty good about now for me as well.

Holding my breath, I watched as Dawn deftly worked us out and around the marina's breakwater. She had done it! We were now out of the marina!

I didn't want to think about having to come back into the marina later. Again, the flying analogy. Taking off was one thing, putting the plane back down on the runway safely was another thing entirely. And, so it went with our boating.

"Let me take command now," Charlie half-pleaded. "It's my boat, and I want to drive her!"

Having Charlie drive just then was the last thing I wanted. We were still around a lot of boating traffic, and many of those boats were smaller sailboats which were being whisked along by the breeze. There was also a much larger motor yacht edging closer to our position. We couldn't have Charlie run into any of them.

"Charlie, how about if Dawn keeps the helm for another few minutes. Maybe we could head across the bay and toward Hat Island," I said, referring to a small, uninhabited island which sat between Anacortes and the mainland. I had hoped Charlie would see the wisdom of this impromptu plan. "When we get out a ways, you can have the boat and put in a lot of boat handling practice."

Charlie reluctantly agreed. This gave Scott and me a wonderful few minutes to sit there in the luxury of the covered fly bridge as we looked out to the awe inspiring scenery all around us.

Cruising along as we were, I eventually remembered that we still had the four fenders hanging along the starboard side of the boat, so I headed down from the fly bridge to retrieve them. I suppose they could have just stayed there, but, to me, it seemed like we should take the fenders in and stow them away.

Whenever I saw a boat cruising along with fenders hanging alongside, it just looked sloppy to me. It was as if the boat's owner was just too lazy to bring them in. As an official co-captain of *Trixie's Destiny*, I didn't want for this beautiful boat to look like that.

This model of Grand Banks Aleutian is wonderful for ease of handling and storing fenders. Perhaps other boats are just as easy, but this was my first personal experience. Working my way forward, I unclipped the first and second fenders from the side railing and found a ready-made storage locker for them, below a forward-facing bench seat.

The third fender was just as easy to unclip. The fourth, not so much. The clip was stuck. I had to reach over and wrestle with it.

I was also in the water. Again.

It would seem that Captain Charlie had taken the controls.

This time, there was no dock nearby, nor were there people on dock to come rushing to my assistance.

It was just me, damn cold water, the fender I had just unclipped, and *Trixie's Destiny* disappearing into the distance.

~ ~ ~ ~ ~ ~

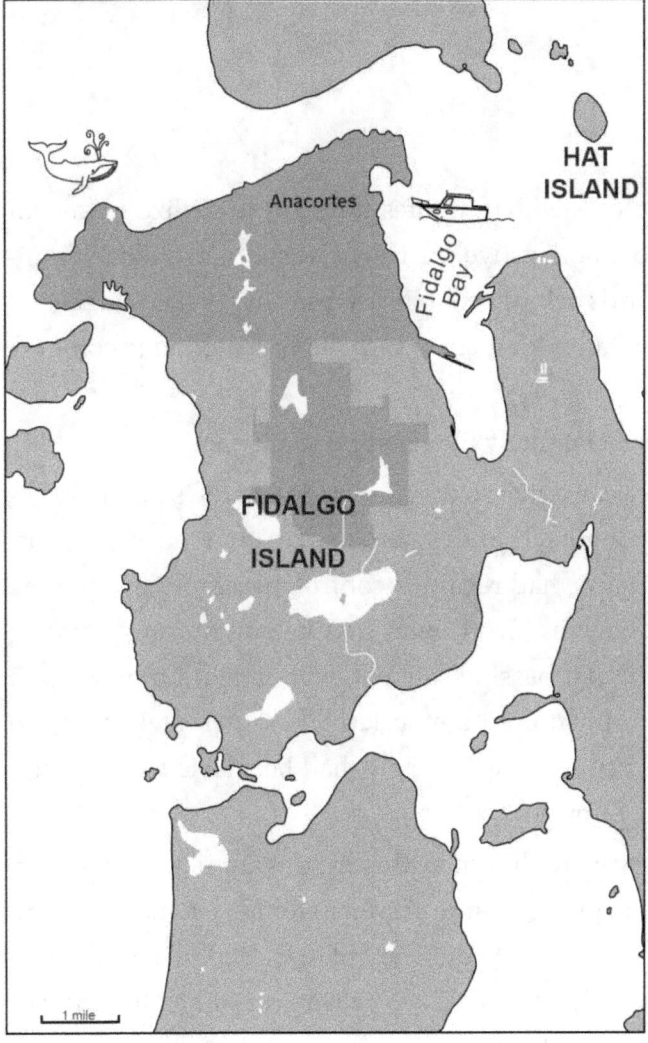

ANACORTES and FIDALGO ISLAND

HAT ISLAND

Anacortes

Fidalgo Bay

FIDALGO ISLAND

1 mile

15: Mutiny Anyone?

It took several minutes for Scott to realize I was not around, another two for Dawn to spot me almost a hundred yards behind, bobbing in the boat's wake, and several more minutes for them to turn the boat around to come get me.

I was definitely not a happy co-captain!

I was also right that it had been Charlie's doing. Without paying heed to the status of his crew of co-captains, once Charlie had regained control, he simply gunned the boat's engines. Scott, who had been admiring a young woman on a passing sailboat, was caught off guard and thrown down onto the deck. He was definitely going to have a bruise. Dawn, luckily, had been able to grab a rail and stay upright.

They were shaken by this. I guess they should have expected it, given Charlie's earlier attempts at maneuvering the boat. Now that I think about it, we should have known this might happen well before we ever turned the engines on. Charlie's driving has always been horrible!

Let me restate that. Charlie's driving just plain sucks! When driving, he knows two speeds, go real fast, stop real quick. Maybe it's a result of all of those years as a fireman. With Charlie driving, the passengers are always a moment away from a case of whiplash and it definitely felt like we were on the way to a fire.

Whatever the cause, Charlie seemed to have transferred his driving style to boating.

It took a lot to get those engines to push one-hundred thousand pounds around, and achieving jackrabbit starts such as Charlie had done, was a bit of a feat. To Charlie, it seemed to come naturally, so, if we ever wanted to participate in a "big-ass yacht race," Charlie would be our captain of choice. Otherwise, I'd choose Dawn.

It wasn't until both Dawn and Scott had settled down and had stopped yelling at Charlie that they wondered where I was. Thankfully, Scott quickly did an onboard search and determined I wasn't to be found. At the same time, Dawn looked in the water. If it wasn't for this quick response on their part, I might have been in that water a whole lot longer. If I hadn't drowned, that is.

I was in the water fully clothed and without a life jacket. I did, thankfully, have the large floating boat fender to hang onto. Otherwise, I would have been in trouble. The nearest land was much further away than I wanted to attempt to swim, even with the fender to keep me afloat.

And, something big swam by me!

Finally, when the boat came up close, Scott came down with a life ring at the ready. Seeing that I had the fender, he set the life ring aside and just watched me, making sure I was okay, while Dawn carefully maneuvered the boat closer.

Charlie had rushed to grab a fire extinguisher but set it aside, seeing that it wasn't needed. I guess, for a retired fireman, having a fire extinguisher to help a drowning man made sense. "There are a lot of them on board," I heard him tell Scott as he set it aside, as if this explained anything.

With the extinguisher and life ring set aside, Scott and Charlie stood on the back swim platform as they reached down to pull me and the fender out of the water.

"Screw this," I thought. I reached up to Charlie's outstretched hand, yanked hard, and pulled him in. He splashed next to me.

That was fantastic!

Retribution complete, I took Scott's hand and worked my way back up into the boat. We both stood there and just stared back at Charlie.

We waited several minutes, watching Charlie sputter and gasp, before helping him back in. I wanted to wait a lot longer, but Scott said no.

As this was going on, Dawn had shut off the engines and come rushing down to us. "Charlie, either you learn how to handle this damn boat, or you will have a mutiny on your hands!" she exclaimed. Actually, it was more of a ticked-off yell. For the first time ever, I saw Dawn almost lose her cool.

"Yeah, mutiny!" I added, as I stood there in the aft deck dripping. Charlie, standing near me, was equally as wet and dripping.

"Crap, just crap," Charlie lamented. "I'm sorry, Frank."

We stood there for several moments as I glared holes into him. I like Charlie, but at that moment I could have punched his lights out.

"Take us back in," Scott said to Dawn. "Looks like more dry clothes are needed, again."

Charlie's eyes lit up. "Actually, I have a surprise for everyone. I should have thought of it the first time Frank dove in, this morning."

"Dove in?" Now, I really wanted to punch him.

Charlie ignored my outburst. "My surprise for each of you just came in late yesterday and I put them in everyone's cabins this morning."

"What are you up to now, Charlie?" Dawn asked, her exasperation showing.

"Go see," he repeated. "Trust me."

"Trust you?" Scott complained. "Charlie, not that we don't love you like a friend and all, but trust is not in the equation right now."

Charlie, seeing that none of us were about to move, relented. "I bought everyone, even me, new uniforms. I thought it would be fun. They're in your cabins."

"If those uniforms are as 'fun' as the wind-breakers and caps you bought before, this ought to be great," Scott said sarcastically.

"Go see," he said simply.

So, we did. Ten minutes later, Charlie and I were back on deck and wearing our new uniforms. Scott and Dawn, not having a need to change, were simply holding theirs in their hands.

I had to admit, Charlie had done just fine. Our new uniforms consisted of casual khaki slacks, a white shirt with my name and co-captain title subtly embossed on it, socks, and even new deck shoes. He had also included another cap for each of us, a good thing as my original co-captain's cap was floating in the bay somewhere.

"You got my size just right. I'm surprised," I stated to Charlie.

"Everyone's sizes should be correct," Charlie responded simply.

"Even mine?" Dawn asked, then seeing Charlie nod in the affirmative, added, "I really don't want to know how you knew what size to get for me."

"I'm good at guessing sizes. It's something I learned from my wife."

"Creepy, Charlie. Your knowing my sizes is really, creepy." Dawn said as she was shaking her head.

So, we were all now dressed in dry clothing again and, luckily, still safe. While all of this was going on, no one had thought to keep a watch out for other boats or navigational hazards. Luckily, we were fine. Out in the open water as we were, we easily could have had an incident with other boats or drifted into the shallows and gotten stuck. None of that happened; a result of sheer luck only.

"Great, now let's eat!" Scott exclaimed.

"Oh, crap on a crutch, I knew I forgot something!"

"What now?" Dawn asked, afraid to hear the answer.

"Food. We don't have any food on board. Sorry,"

Scott just glared at Charlie. "I swear, I will throw your lottery-winning ass overboard one of these days!"

~ ~ ~ ~ ~ ~

16: A Bit of Training

"You're getting better!" I complimented Charlie. He needed the praise. Ever since he'd acquired *Trixie's Destiny*, Charlie had taken one ding after another to his ego.

"Yes, and I'm sorry about before," he repeated.

We were again seated in McDuck's Coffee Bar. This time for lunch. A much-needed late lunch, and we were starved.

After learning there wasn't any food on board, Scott and I had wanted to just head back to the marina, about twenty minutes away, and give up for the day, maybe even give up on this yachting thing completely. Dawn, on the other hand, wasn't ready to walk away from this so quickly.

She persuaded us to remain out in the bay awhile longer so we could each get in some boat-handling experience. So, we did, and she was right. Starting with Charlie, we each took turns at the fly bridge helm, trying different maneuvers; starts, turns, sideways maneuvers with the thrusters, backing up, and then doing it all again.

We pretended that one log floating in the water was a marina and we each took turns to line up to it, as if we were going to dock. Doing it this way wasn't at all intimidating.

Dawn, it turned out, was an incredible teacher.

Charlie, unfortunately, was the worst of the four of us, but he was showing some improvement. In another decade or so, I might trust him to dock the boat on his own.

For now, Dawn was our designated marina and docking expert. As I had seen before, maneuvering the yacht just came naturally to her and I let her know it.

"I paid attention in class," she said simply, when I complimented her as we had lunch there in McDuck's.

"I thought she was just paying attention to the dad of those two kids," Scott bravely teased.

The interesting thing here, again, was Dawn's response. She was actually blushing. Who knew that there was a female somewhere inside that hard-as-nails, former detective?

"We—Tony and I—are going out to dinner, tomorrow," Dawn said sheepishly.

"You and the dad?" Scott exclaimed.

"Yep, now shut up about it or you will end up talking in a much higher octave." She had used that threat before. None of us dared test her resolve to follow through.

"You'll give us full details and all, won't you?" Scott bravely retorted.

"One more, Scott. One more," she taunted him with a fork pointed toward his leg.

Despite being dumped into the water twice within a few hours, the day had actually been rather fun. We now all had a bit more confidence and felt like we might actually be able to handle the boat.

I reflected back on my flying lessons, though. Lessons that I never finished, so I never got my pilot's license. When I took those lessons, it didn't take all that long to learn the basics of handling a small airplane. Taking off, taxiing, landing approaches, and so on. What did take long was everything else: emergency procedures, radio, navigation, more navigation, rules and regulations.

This boating thing was incredibly similar. We were starting to learn how to physically handle the boat, but we had zero experience in every other aspect of this.

Somehow, my worry about all of the other stuff was fading. After today, I felt we could learn those other things. Not all at once, but it would eventually come.

"We need food and such on board. At least enough for a lunch or two, if we are going to go back out tomorrow," Dawn said. She then wrote out a list and handed it to Charlie.

"Here, oh mighty captain, you go buy all of this stuff, stock it onboard *Trixie*, and I might actually come back on board.

Charlie accepted the list and tucked it in his shirt pocket.

"Yeah, Charlie," Scott attempted his own half-assed threat. "No food. No co-captains."

"You guys will go out with me again, even after today?" Charlie was obviously pleased by this.

"You showed potential during maneuver training out on the water today," Dawn responded. "If you promise to not be a jerk again and learn with the rest of us how to manage *Trixie's Destiny*, then, yes, we will come back on board."

"But, don't forget the food!" I added.

~ ~ ~ ~ ~ ~

17: Whale Bait

I loved this!

Taking a handsome, sturdy yacht like *Trixie's Destiny* out beyond the bay and into the Puget Sound, the feel and smell of the cool, salty air. Views of snow-capped mountains in several directions. The sight of beautiful yachts of all sizes, and the wonderful, old Washington State ferries cruising nearby.

It can't get better than this.

We had three days of our own personally-crafted yacht training under our belt. Since our first excursion, two additional training days had been completed, each time in the bay between Fidalgo Island and Hat Island. We took time to learn every aspect of the boat. Made test calls with the radio. Reviewed basic rights-of-way when on the water and learned the basics of the navigation system. Then, we pulled out our manuals from the training down in Everett and reviewed what the markers on the numerous buoys meant. This had been confusing to us all. We even tried out the stabilizer and learned how to lower the tender into the water and raise it back up.

Charlie, being a retired firefighter, was a nut for safety drills. I rather liked this, and I was happy to report to my wife how much safety training we were doing.

Given our lack of experience, it was good to know that our chances of staying alive were a bit better. One drill he had us do was to pretend there was a fire in the galley. We totally screwed it up as no one knew what to do. Charlie then made sure that each of us knew our roles and we did it again. The second time was better. After this, we conducted a similar drill, pretending there was a fire in the engine room. This time, we were great. At the end of the drill, there were three of us standing in the engine room holding fire extinguishers, Charlie again marveled at the large number of extinguishers on board.

So, well, we might not go down in flames after all.

After the on-the-water self-training, we braved a trip over to the marina's fuel center and found more help than we could ever want. At that center, and with a multitude of "old salts" gleefully giving us their advice, we learned the basics of refueling the yacht, how to connect up electricity when in port, how to add new fresh water, and even how to pump out the bilge and other unmentionables; I think it is called "grey water and black water."

We were now much more familiar with the yacht, and we felt ready to go out for a real adventure. So, on our fourth day, we headed out toward Decatur Island, our first big journey. Decatur Island is one of the closer, and less developed, islands in the San Juan chain, and nowhere near as popular as the better known Orcas Island and Friday Harbor.

Being here, on this sturdy yacht, heading out on a day's adventure, was an absolute, sensual delight; it was what yachting should be all about.

Except now, for the third time since leaving Anacortes and Fidalgo Bay, Captain Charlie was at the stern, heaving his guts out.

Man was he green around the gills!

The distance from the marina in Anacortes to Decatur Island is only around fifteen miles. About an hour's cruise each way at moderate speed. This might not seem like a lot, but for us, it was a huge deal. Leaving our protected bay and going out into "real water" was like the first time you rode a bike without training wheels.

Our ultimate goal was to go into "blue water" and, hopefully, even up to Alaska or down to Oregon.

Five minutes out of the bay and rounding the top of Fidalgo Island to head west, the water grew a bit rougher and Charlie grew greener.

Ten minutes out of the bay, Charlie's breakfast came up, and over the aft it went.

Fifteen minutes out, and I'd swear he was hacking up his spleen.

How could one man's stomach have held so much? Well, he was in need of a diet; I guess this was one way to do it.

I went into the galley, which was now partially stocked, and looked around. There had to be something to help Charlie. If he was going to be so miserable, this whole yachting thing just wasn't going to work. It wasn't like Scott, Dawn and I could take the yacht out and leave Charlie behind. So, it was in our best interest to see if we could help him.

Ginger. The moment my eyes fell on a bag of ginger in the small pantry, which had been picked up from Whole Foods along with a whole variety of other edibles, I knew we had a likely solution.

Charlie had tried Dramamine. A mistake, but he wouldn't listen to us. All Dramamine seems to do is make you groggy and feel useless. Nibbling on ginger, however, was a great way to quickly perk up.

I went to the aft section of the boat and looked at our poor, green captain. Dawn was nearby to make sure he was safe. I showed her the ginger package and she immediately agreed.

Charlie nibbled on it, and then sat back on one of the seats in the covered cockpit. Wow, but he looked miserable! He chewed on the ginger, having been forced to do so by Dawn. Then he sat there and just groaned. I think he had hoped for an immediate, miracle cure. That wasn't going to happen. He would just get a whole lot better, not totally cured.

I sat with Dawn as we made small talk with Charlie, trying to take his mind off of his current condition. Scott was in the pilothouse, navigating *Trixie's Destiny* toward our goal. He kept the yacht at a slow twelve knots and had engaged the stabilizer, a device which did wonders to reduce the seasick-making roll of a boat. Apparently, it still wasn't enough to keep Charlie's breakfast down though.

"Whales to port!" We all heard Scott's voice over the speaker. The speakers were one of the systems we had learned to use, and it was incredibly handy as it helped us communicate with each other throughout the multi-deck boat.

I leaned out and looked to the port side. Nothing.

"Maybe, they're on the other port side," Charlie said.

Holy poop deck, our captain was actually attempting a joke. Maybe he was getting better. At least, it might have been a joke. When it came to Charlie and the port-starboard thing, you never knew for sure.

Whales are commonly seen in this area, but they are always exciting to view. Now that we were out on the water with them, it would be all the more fun.

Dawn grabbed her cellphone and turned on the camera function. To be able to see them better, we both scurried up the back set of stairs to the fly bridge.

Still nothing.

Scott had said they were on the port side so I focused my attention there while Dawn watched the starboard side.

"I'll reposition so that you can get a better view," I heard Scott announce over the yacht-wide speaker system.

BUMP!

"What the heck was that?" I exclaimed, just as Scott made a hard turn to starboard.

"We hit something! A whale?" Dawn responded worried.

I glanced down into the water to see if I could spot an injured whale, or hopefully, just an errant log. I didn't see either.

What I did see was Charlie in the cold water, and he was waving his arms frantically about.

Then, I did finally see a whale and it was headed right for Charlie!

"Charlie, look behind you!" I called out frantically, pointing to where we could see the backside of a whale. It was less than sixty yards from Charlie and coming closer.

Both Dawn and I ran back down to the aft deck. She grabbed a life ring with *Trixie's Destiny* emblazoned on it, while I grabbed a rope in preparation to toss to Charlie so we could reel him in.

Then Charlie saw the whale and I would swear his scream sounded just like my sister's, back when she was ten years old.

I wish I had recorded it. It would have been fun to playback at parties.

The whale, having no interest in Charlie, ambled on, passing within thirty feet of him. It would seem that Charlie was not going to be whale bait. At least, not today.

~ ~ ~ ~ ~ ~

18: Back in the Water

It turns out we had bumped into a log. Thankfully.

I would hate to think that our boat had been instrumental in killing or injuring one of the magnificent whales that populated the waters here.

Killing a log... no problem. Killing a whale... big problem.

There are many logs floating in the waters in the Puget Sound, we had simply found one of them and it had scared each of us. I can only guess what banging into a large object like that would do to a smaller boat. It certainly was felt on Charlie's sixty-five footer.

So, our attention needed to be placed on our sodden captain. After Dawn and I reeled Charlie back onto the boat, our shaken captain stood there dripping from head to toe.

"That sucker was going to eat me!" Charlie whimpered.

"Nah, you're too ugly," I teased him.

Charlie patted his head and then quickly looked around. "My captain's hat! It's gone!"

"No, Charlie, it isn't," Dawn said, handing it to him. "It was right here on the deck."

"How'd you get dumped over, anyway?" I asked.

"I wanted to see the whales, too," he whined. "You two were on the top deck, so I just leaned out to see if I could spot one. That's when Scott jerked the boat and dumped me in!"

"He did it to keep from banging into other logs. Seems there were quite a few of them ahead of us," Dawn defended Scott. She had gone forward to the pilothouse and obtained a report from him.

"Oh. I guess that's okay. Don't want to bang up my yacht."

"Speaking of which, let's check her out," I led Charlie and Dawn up to the forepeak. One great thing about Grand Banks yachts is the ease of moving about on the outer side decks. Getting access to the front was simple.

I signaled for Scott to come to a stop and he did. I didn't want to accidentally fall in at the bow of the boat, only to be run over.

With both Charlie and Dawn holding on to me, I leaned way over and studied the front of the yacht. We were okay. The log hadn't damaged her. I didn't even see a noteworthy scratch.

Then I was in the water!

Son of a bitch! This was getting to be ridiculous.

Immediately, Dawn found and tossed out another life ring which I easily caught. I was starting to get used to this.

"Sorry, Frank," I heard Charlie's voice. "I had to sneeze."

Again, I was ready to punch his lights out.

This was my third frigging time to get dumped in, and I didn't like it anymore now than I did the first time.

Clutching the life ring, I slowly worked my way around to the stern while sputtering obscenities all of the way.

As I climbed up the ass-end of the yacht, I heard Dawn caution me.

"Don't, Frank," she pleaded as she saw the deadly look in my eyes. "My hands slipped too. It's both of our faults."

I said nothing. Not caring if I was dripping salt water all through Charlie's expensive yacht, I worked my way through the main salon, through the pilothouse, then down to my cabin. I had chosen the smaller mid-cabin.

Somehow, I had a feeling something like this might happen. I had another complete change of clothes on board now as a "just in case" thing, in addition to the extra uniform brought on by Charlie. Good thing too, the extra clothes clearly were needed.

I still wanted to punch Charlie's lights out.

~ ~ ~ ~ ~ ~

19: Family Day

The four of us were nervous but were trying to not let it show.

Captain Charlie proudly stood on the dock at the starboard-side entrance to *Trixie's Destiny* where we had a set of wooden steps to enable easy entrance up into the yacht. Scott, Dawn and I stood alongside, playing the role of a professional crew. We were all wearing our tidy new uniforms, windbreakers emblazoned with our names, and shiny new Co-Captain caps.

We each had several uniforms now. Given our proclivity for being dumped unceremoniously into the water, Charlie thought it wise for us to have back-ups. I would rather have stayed dry but given the likelihood of being dumped into the water at frequent intervals, having a supply of dry uniforms on board made sense.

In the small hanging closet in my cabin, I now had four caps and three windbreakers with the title "Co-Captain" emblazoned on them.

I was actually growing rather fond of the co-captain title, even though there supposedly was no such thing and it was a bit of a joke between us. I just didn't want to wear the cap with that title out in public.

A young woman in a white catering uniform was standing on deck to greet each person as they boarded, ready to hand out mimosas to the adults and sodas to those under twenty-one. Charlie had hired a caterer for this special occasion. We, and our guests, were to be afforded first-class service on this special day.

It was family day!

We now had another week of experience under our belt, and Captain Charlie was finally able to go on an excursion without hurling his guts, so he had declared that the upcoming Saturday would be family day; a day for each of us to invite our families to take a journey on *Trixie*.

This event was important to me, thus my nervousness. I wanted everything to be perfect. I wanted for my wife, Francine, to appreciate all that we had learned. Gaining her acceptance and praise was important to me.

And, there was the constant screw-up thing. Lord knows we'd had bungled enough so far, I didn't want for this to be one of those days. Not with family and friends on board.

Coming up the dock toward us, was my wife, our daughter and her husband, and our grand-daughter.

Behind them, I saw Scott's wife, Sally, and their son, a lawyer who practiced in nearby Burlington.

Another half-dozen people came up to the long floating concrete dock to join us for the event including Mac, the owner of McDuck's Coffee Bar. Charlie had also invited Amanda Amund, the widow of Roger Amund, the boat's previous owner.

I didn't know most of the others, which was no surprise given that we had each sent out our own invitations. The last four to come on board were Tony Drew — the man who had been in training with us — his twin sons and some guy I didn't know.

There were nearly twenty people on board, including us, and the two caterers. *Trixie* was more than large enough to accommodate all of these people for our grand adventure. We were going to do some whale watching. Word was, a new pod of orcas had moved in, so we should have some good sightings.

Actually, I didn't care if we saw fifty whales or zero. What I did care about was having a good, safe voyage and one where Charlie, Scott, Dawn and I didn't come across as total screw-ups.

It didn't help that Charlie had billed this as a "Three-Hour Tour." It would seem that he had never watched *Gilligan's Island*, whose infamous "three-hour tour" had lasted years.

Odd thing was, Charlie totally reminded me of the skipper on *Gilligan's Island* and Dawn sort of looked like an older Mary Ann. Interesting, now that I think of it, given that the actress' real name was Dawn Wells. Two "Dawns," both of them intelligent, attractive and confident women.

Setting aside thoughts of *Gilligan's Island*, I turned my attention to the day and to our boating adventure. For starters, we had good weather, a great omen for our voyage. What mattered most was how we totally shined. Our hours of practice showed. Dawn took the helm for our departure, going through her checklist, while Charlie, Scott and I managed the lines and fenders, and did it in such a way that we actually looked like we knew what we were doing.

The day was perfect. So far, anyway.

With the lines and fenders on board, and the boat safely on its way, Charlie went topside to navigate. He was actually getting to be pretty good at navigation while Dawn remained the superior boat handler in our team. Not a bad division of duties, actually. What mattered most right now was to give the appearance of Charlie being in control. His directing the course of the boat did exactly that while having Dawn drive ensured that we wouldn't bump into anything in the process.

Scott and I spent a bit of time making sure everyone was happy. They loved it! Various invitees were sitting and relaxing throughout the boat, and the caterers were doing a wonderful job as they served drinks and munchies. My wife, our daughter and her family were totally enthralled and soon were encamped on the comfortable, covered seating on the fly bridge, adjacent to the upper helm and the best seats on the yacht.

The two young boys from our training down in Everett, Tony Drew's sons, were up at the prow, excitedly pointing out the many sights, landmarks and other boats. I didn't see their father, but assumed he was nearby.

I was holding my breath. So far, we hadn't killed anyone, bumped into anything, dumped anyone overboard, and no one was seasick, not even Captain Charlie.

Charlie was given control of the boat once we were out of the marina and he took us out into the channel as we turned north, and then west, with our goal being the stretch of water between Fidalgo and Lopez islands. We had done this before and Charlie knew the way. There was a fair bit of other boating traffic, but we had all learned how to thread our way through them, even the good Captain.

Thankfully, the seas were calm. Still, we had the stabilizer kicked into gear. We didn't want Charlie, or any of our guests, to become seasick.

After a while, I went up and retrieved my wife, Francine, so that I could give her a full tour of the lower decks. I wanted to show off every aspect of *Trixie's Destiny*. We had been dusting and scrubbing the yacht and she was in perfect condition to show off.

Francine loved the interior of the boat with its warm wood charm. We started with a tour of the pilothouse and neighboring galley, and then I took her to the lower deck to tour the three cabins, each with their own head. I let her poke her head into every cabin and head, and other nooks such as the laundry. Then we headed back up, and I was able to show her the impressive features in the pilot house and galley. This done, we went out and aft to the cockpit where several of our guests were relaxing, watching the sights and enjoying the catered service.

No whale sightings yet, but everyone on board was primed with cameras at the ready.

Francine and I encountered Mac and I told him that I was about to show my wife the engine room. Soon, he was joining in on this little adventure, although I wasn't sure how well, with his bulk, he could navigate the steep wooden steps down to that aft area. Two others also asked to come. Seeing the engine room, and doing so while the engines were operating, would be a treat.

So, as a group of five, we made our way down into the lower crew area, which would then enable us to enter the engine room.

That is when I, and the whole group of us, found Dawn playing kissy-face with Tony Drew, the father of the two boys.

If I'd had doubted before that Dawn had a thing for Tony Drew, that uncertainty quickly vanished.

Wow, was she embarrassed! She and Tony had been so into one another that they had not tuned into the fact that a group of people were approaching. When they did see us, boy did they jump!

The wonderful thing about this, even though it cost Dawn a few embarrassment points, was my wife was able to see Dawn with another guy. We had some big overnight boating adventures ahead of us, and I would be doing so with Dawn on board. For my wife to know that Dawn was interested in another man, any other man, was a great relief to her.

Still, you should have seen the look on Dawn's embarrassed face. It was priceless!

Trying to make light of the situation, I guided my small tour group into the engine room and away from Dawn and Tony as they tried to compose themselves back in the cramped crew area.

The engine room was surprisingly loud, now that we were underway, and I had opened the door. The fact that you could not hear the engines outside of the engine room was a testament to how well insulated it was.

Even with the noise, my little tour group appreciated that they were able to see it, and I was happy to show off this area, and take some of the attention off of Dawn.

No such luck. The attention was still on Dawn and her amorous activities; she was definitely one of the highlights of the day.

The others, including Tony, left the engine room and crew area to head back up the steep wooden stairs and out to the portside deck. I stayed behind to make sure that everything in the engine room was closed up and secure.

That might have been a mistake. The next thing I knew, I had a gun in my face and an angry looking stranger was glaring at me.

~ ~ ~ ~ ~ ~

20: Where is It?

A gun was pointed at me, and the guy doing so had one of those scary looks, like he could actually pull the trigger.

Not that I had ever seen that look in real life before...just in the movies. I had not had anyone point a gun at me since I'd played cops-and-robbers as a kid and in my aborted stint in ROTC. As a kid, my brother was using a BB gun, and that was scary enough, and in ROTC we only used blanks. I doubted this guy was only armed with BBs or blanks.

"Where is it?" he demanded as we stood there in the short hall between the engine room and the crew quarters—Dawn's quarters.

"What? What are you talking about, and please don't point that thing at me?" What I didn't want to say to the guy was how close I was to peeing my pants.

"Just tell me where it is!"

Again, with this totally meaningless command.

"A few more clues would be helpful," I added, trying to stall.

KLUNK. The man fell to the floor.

Dawn, who had been in the crew-quarters head, her designated area, had been trying to regain her composure when this all started to happen just on the opposite side of the wall. She immediately knew something was wrong and didn't hesitate in correcting the situation.

Cautiously stepping out of the head and grabbing one of the ubiquitous fire extinguishers, she crept up behind the bad guy, managing to nail him on the back of the head with the blunt, heavy, red object.

The bad guy's eyes rolled back into his head and I saw him simply drop. I'd never seen that before. At least, not in real life.

Dawn took over. I went into the head on wobbly legs and took deep breaths, afraid I was about to puke.

"Frank, go get Scott," she commanded me. "Unless, of course, you would rather be a wuss and just throw up right where you stand."

That did it. I didn't want to totally lose what few "guy points" I could muster just then. I took another deep breath, darted up the stairway to the portside walkway, and quickly worked my way up to the fly bridge in search of Scott. I found him sitting with his wife, Sally.

He could see by the look on my face that something was wrong.

"Who fell overboard, this time?"

I can't blame him for asking that. Getting dumped into the cold waters of the Puget Sound was something of a common theme with us.

"Not that. A gun!" I said panting, but in a quiet voice so only he could hear me.

"Slow down. What about a gun?"

I really wasn't doing well in the "staying calm" department, so I had to take another few breaths. Finally, I was able to tell Scott what had happened.

Again, I saw Scott go into cop mode and do so in a heartbeat. He told me to follow along and the two of us made our way back down to the engine room, while trying to act calm, so we wouldn't upset any of our guests. Once there, we found Dawn standing over the bad guy with the gun in her hand, pointing it at him.

"I don't know who this piece-of-crap is, but he isn't any friend of ours," Dawn clarified.

"I saw him come on board with the others," I said. "I assumed he had been invited by one of you."

"Not me," Dawn declared.

"Me neither," Scott added.

This left only Charlie as a possibility. Or, one of our invited guests could have asked him to come along.

The man started to moan, and Dawn commanded him to stand up. Seeing the formidable look in her eyes, he didn't hesitate and slowly worked his way up from the floor. Scott then jerked him up and held him firmly. No one could get out of that grip.

"Guys, what's going on down there?" We heard Charlie's voice come over the ship's intercom. Somehow, he had been alerted to this problem that was occurring two decks below him.

Dawn quickly picked up a small handset so that the communication would be private and not broadcast to all of the others on board. She brought Charlie up to speed on what was happening.

This done, we turned our attention to the bad guy.

"I think it's the same creep who was spying on us from the dock when we first were checking out *Trixie's Destiny*!" Dawn exclaimed. She looked through the photos on her cellphone and found one she had taken of him, thinking it was just a joke at the time. "Same guy," she said simply as she showed the photo to Scott and me.

Scott shoved him down onto the bed in the crew area. Dawn's bed. He looked scared and mad.

"Who are you?" Scott demanded.

He just shook his head in response, so Scott roughly grabbed at the man to search through his pockets. Surprisingly, he found a wallet and an ID.

"Viktor Jairo," Scott read aloud to us. "From Colombia."

"Colombia, oh just freaking great!" Dawn exclaimed. "Don't tell me that we have some sort of drug thing going on now!"

"Wait!" I said. "I know that name!" I turned to our bad guy, captive. "Weren't you the captain of this boat before? When Roger Amund was killed?" This name had a familiar ring. Perhaps it was something Charlie had said at one point.

His look told me I was right. He still wouldn't say anything.

"Give me a moment," I told Scott and Dawn as I left the crew area and went in search of Amanda Amund. It didn't take long; she was in the covered aft sitting area, not far from the doorway.

I went to Amanda and pulled her aside so that our conversation would be private. When I told her the name, Viktor Jairo, she confirmed my suspicions. Our captive was the previous captain. Interesting.

Back down in the crew area, I told the other two what I had learned.

"So, Captain Jairo, just what is it that brings you back to *Trixie's Destiny*?" Dawn asked him.

No response.

"Please let me rough him up. Pretty please!" Scott pleaded.

I didn't know if Scott was serious or not.

Dawn would have nothing to do with it. I was on Scott's side. After all, this guy had just poked a gun in my face.

"Where is it?" The guy, Viktor, finally spoke up.

"Where is what?" Scott asked.

"That's all he kept asking me," I told them. "Seems he thinks we know where something of note is."

"Drugs?" Dawn grilled Viktor.

The man simply shook his head.

"Did you kill Roger Amund?" Scott joined in the grilling.

"No! I am not a killer!"

"Well, then. If you say you aren't a killer, we'll totally believe that," Scott retorted sarcastically.

"You're the guy who broke into the boat a while back and hit Charlie. Aren't you?" Dawn barked at the man.

"Charlie?" The name obviously meant nothing to him.

"The guy who came onto the boat and you hit him," Dawn said in explanation.

"I didn't want to hurt him. He surprised me, that's all."

That was one mystery solved, at least.

"What are you looking for? What is it that you think is on this boat? If not drugs, what?" Dawn tossed these questions at him rapidly.

"Not drugs. If you don't know, it is better that you don't."

"Why," Scott asked.

"That's all I have to say. I want off of this boat."

We totally wanted this jerk off of our boat as well. The question was how.

Dawn, Scott and I conferred about this for a bit. We had several options. We could simply go back to port, turn him over to the police and ruin all of our guests' day in the process. Or, we could tie him up and keep his presence secret from the others but put everyone in jeopardy if something went wrong with this plan and he escaped. Or, the option we chose, we could call the Coast Guard and see if they would come out and retrieve him.

Scott and I went up topside to talk with Charlie and told him what our thoughts were. He agreed.

This was where another aspect of our training came into play: dealing with emergencies and emergency agencies over the marine radio. In this case, the Coast Guard.

Charlie slowed the boat to a crawl and then handled the communication with the Coast Guard like a pro. Probably because he is one. His years as a firefighter gave him substantial experience in this sort of thing. Even with my previous flight training and a few communications with the control tower, I would have fumbled it. Within moments, Charlie had the call completed and said they were on their way.

They were impressive and wasted no time with unnecessary questions. Once Charlie described the situation, they immediately went into action, dispatching one of their Rapid Response Boats out from the Anacortes station. Knowing they were on the way was a relief. All we had to do now was keep Viktor at bay as we waited for the Coast Guard boat to arrive.

It took less time than even the Coast Guard dispatcher said it would. Those folks are organized. In less time than I would have believed possible, a swift orange and white boat was in sight and racing toward us.

Charlie brought *Trixie's Destiny* to a halt and the Coast Guard crew expertly came alongside. Soon we had three of them onboard. Charlie had alerted everyone as to what was going on and they all knew to stand aside and let the Coast Guard do their thing. This certainly didn't keep them from pulling out their cameras and capturing the event.

I wondered how long it would be before this arrest showed up on the local news. My guess was that videos were being streamed to the local TV station or to YouTube as it was happening.

Within a few minutes, they had Viktor out from the lower deck of our boat and onto their boat. The transfer was easy and hassle free. You could tell that this was not the first time they had done something like this. They knew what they were doing.

One of the officers took our statements and we were asked to come into the Coast Guard station once our day's whale watching adventure was done. We all agreed.

I liked the fact that he didn't even blink an eye when Scott, Dawn and I each introduced ourselves as co-captains.

Dawn was concerned there might be illegal drugs on board and she told the leader of the Coast Guard detail this. He pondered this situation for a bit and then called to his superior officer. I feared that, given the potential of illegal drugs, our boat might be hauled in immediately. Luckily, this didn't happen. What did happen was that two of the officers took a long tour of *Trixie's Destiny* to see if they could find anything. They didn't, and, given no evidence of drugs, they let us go.

They did remind us rather firmly to bring the boat in at the end of our boating trip so they could bring a drug-detecting dog on board. We were happy to oblige.

Well, that certainly added an unexpected twist to the day.

Now, we just had to figure out what "it" was that Viktor was looking for, and if "it" was still on board. Hopefully the drug-sniffing dog would resolve this for us.

If drugs were found, would *Trixie's Destiny* be confiscated or impounded? That thought worried each of us.

Luckily, the tone of the day turned positive again when one of the boys called out to everyone that he could see whales.

Soon, nearly everyone onboard was looking for them, and no one was disappointed. We were surrounded by them!

The event with Viktor had almost ruined our outing, but with the whale sighting, everything was good and fun again.

People pay good money for this sort of tour, and I was thrilled that our "three-hour tour" had turned out so well and so many whales had come up nearby.

If it wasn't for that gun and "it" thing that Viktor had been looking for, the whole day would have been perfect.

UPPER PUGET SOUND

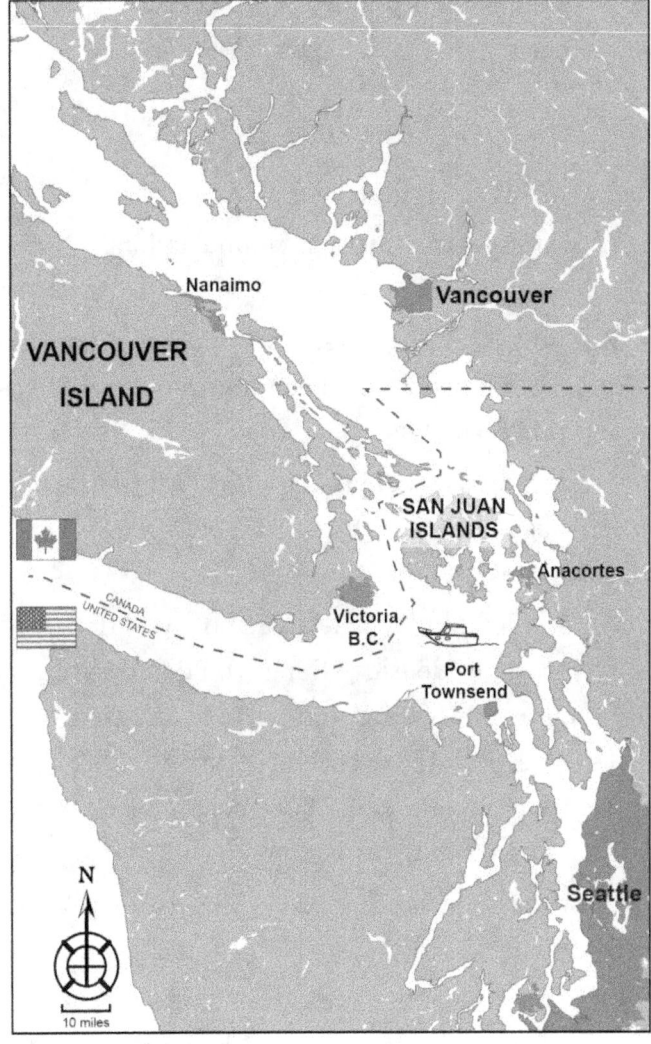

21: Crossing the Sound

The Coast Guard's drug dog found nothing. Thankfully.

Still, this left a big mystery. What had Viktor been looking for? Someone had been murdered for "it," and this worried each of us.

Charlie was a mix of pissed, worried and curious. His anxiety was growing. As for the rest of us, we just wanted to figure out what the hell was going on.

We decided to play detective and try to find out. At the very least, the detective thing would add some fun to this whole new yachting thing. It would also give us a great excuse to take an overnight jaunt on *Trixie's Destiny*. Our first. Up until now, all of our boating had been for a few hours here and there during the day.

This was about to change, and we were all looking forward to it.

Port Townsend. A scenic, historic town across the Puget Sound was our destination. I had only been there once; I'd taken a ferry over from Whidbey Island with

Francine. We stayed in a quaint Bed-and-Breakfast while there and spent a quiet day roaming through the shops and exploring nearby Fort Worden, a retired military base that had been converted into a state park.

I would totally do it again, and this boating trip of ours would seem to be accomplishing much of that. Except, I wouldn't be with my wife and our "B and B" would be the yacht instead of an old inn.

Now, our foursome's first overnight trip on *Trixie's Destiny* was about to happen. By our best calculations, it would take about three hours to cross the Sound to get to the Port Townsend Boat Haven Marina at moderate speed. We could probably have done a round trip in one day, but it was time for us to gain the experience of spending a night or two on the boat.

I remember when a great adventure involved hiking, camping in tents, and having to fish for our dinner. Now, it seems that going on an adventure meant sitting back in luxury on a yacht, sleeping in a comfortable and private cabin and choosing if we wanted to eat on the boat or at a local restaurant.

Port Townsend was not only a great boating trip and adventure for us, but it was also where Roger Amund had been killed.

When Roger had owned *Trixie's Destiny*, it had been berthed there. Roger also kept a long-term berth rental at the Everett Marina, closer to where he lived with his wife, Amanda.

We learned from Amanda that she had not even known of the Port Townsend berth until her husband had died. Another mystery and another fact pointing to that town as a place to do our detective thing.

Having two long-term slips was odd, although I had heard of others who did the same thing; always to the displeasure of the other boaters. Some yacht owners dubbed them "slip hogs," and I couldn't blame them. Berths for larger boats, like *Trixie's Destiny*, could be hard to come by and there were often long waiting lists for them; keeping more than one berth was just plain selfish.

Whatever the reason, Roger had a long-term berth at Port Townsend, and he had been killed while the boat was in that berth. To be more precise, he had been shot as he sat on the john while at that berth.

Not a glamorous way to die.

We called ahead and learned that the slip was still under contract and was open for us to use. Amanda had not known to cancel it, so there were four more months prepaid on the slip rental. Great. We had a place to head to and stay overnight.

In our calls with the Port Townsend marina, we learned that Roger had hired a local yacht-management firm to watch over *Trixie's Destiny* and keep her maintained and clean when she was in port. It was one of the people from this cleaning team who had found him.

Charlie had hired a similar firm in Anacortes. Services like these made the life of a yacht owner far easier. It was little things like wiping the boat down and cleaning it and servicing the engines that made life so much better. This way, when the yacht owner wanted to go out for a day, the boat would be clean, the outside seating dry and free of seagull poop, the water tanks full, and the holding tanks clean. All the yacht owner had to do was fire up the engines and have fun taking the boat out.

In preparation for our journey, we each had brought on board enough clothing for several nights, even though we were planning on just one night. We wanted the flexibility, should we decide to stay out a bit longer.

Charlie had also purchased enough food to keep us fed for a week. Stocking *Trixie's Destiny* with all of this had required multiple trips from his SUV in the marina parking lot, down the long dock, and finally out to the boat, each of us with arms full of food supplies. It wasn't until much later that we learned the marina had a golf cart we could have used. We realized that on the last journey, with arms loaded, as the marina's golf cart hummed by, loaded with supplies for a different yacht.

I felt a little guilty about being so excited at the prospect of this overnight trip, even though we had talked about taking long trips right from the beginning. My guilt was due to this being just the second time I would be away from Francine overnight since I had retired. The first time was when our group of four had spent two nights in Everett while we were taking the boating training and safety course.

Back in our working days, business travel was common and Francine and I had been used to one or the other of us being on the road several nights each month. Now, that had all stopped. Since retiring, any travel we did was done together.

Except, now that I was a member of the *Trixie's Destiny* crew, our plans were to take many overnight trips. I was rather looking forward to it.

I would be spending my nights on board in my little mid-ship cabin that was furnished with a set of twin beds. To me, this was more exciting than if I were planning on staying at the Ritz. Charlie had the large owner's suite; the size of that suite is probably larger than the other cabins combined. Scott had the second largest cabin, dubbed the "VIP" cabin. I had passed on that one when we had gone through the cabin selection process. While bigger, anyone in that forward cabin would be more prone to feeling the up-and-down movement of the boat. No, the little mid-ship cabin I had selected was just fine. That left the crew cabin in the aft of the boat, and Dawn seemed to enjoy having this as her private sanctuary. Private, that is, when there wasn't a group of people on tour coming by just as she was playing kissy-face with Tony.

With each of us moved into our cabins, we set out from Anacortes on a typical Puget Sound day. Drizzle.

The weather was a bummer, but we didn't let it stop us. If we did let a little rain hamper us in that part of the world, we would never be able to take the yacht out. It really only meant that we would be navigating the boat from the interior helm in the pilothouse, and not our preferred location up top on the fly bridge. Not a bad tradeoff.

An interesting aspect of boating occurred to me as we ventured further away from land. The boat felt smaller. Much smaller. When we were in the marina, *Trixie's Destiny* seemed huge, even though there were several other yachts much larger than ours. Now that we were out on open water, she seemed downright tiny and fragile. I could only wonder what it would be like if we were to head out from the Sound and into open ocean...blue water.

An hour into the trip, passing west of the Whidbey Island Naval Air Station, the wind picked up, blowing in from the Strait of Juan de Fuca creating choppy water. For the first time, we were really feeling the movement of the boat.

This also meant that Charlie shouldn't have had so many McBeignets. He had brought in a box of them in the morning and had been munching on the delicious brown morsels from the start of our trip. A huge mistake.

Trixie bobbled along on course. Charlie's stomach was doing its own bit of rocking-and-rolling.

Those McBeignets were soon spewing forth from Charlie in an impressive projectile manner. Luckily, all of it landed in the water. Still, our captain was not doing well, and no amount of ginger to chew on was about to douse those woes.

Two hours into the trip, Charlie was, again, puking out internal organs. Impressive to watch, in its own weird way.

Scott, Dawn and I took turns watching over him as he lay in agony on the padded bench seat in the aft cockpit. Just being around him made the rest of us queasy as well, but no one else got sick. Only our leader, Captain Charlie, seemed to be susceptible to the rolling motions of the boat.

What if we had actually been out on blue water, those bodies of water out from protected areas such as the Sound? How would Charlie do then?

Thankfully, Port Townsend was eventually in sight. I had been at the helm, a role I was totally enjoying, and was able to tell the others over the boat's intercom that we were nearing the peninsula. Luckily, we also were leaving the rough water as we rounded land and headed toward the marina.

Charlie, no doubt, was anxious to be able to step off of the boat and onto dry, unmoving, land.

For me, I was sorry to see this leg of the trip come to a close. I had enjoyed it. Other than Charlie being so ill, it was what I had dreamed that yachting should be; fun and relaxing, salt air, beautiful scenery, including Olympic National Park to the west, sights of other boats passing us, sounds of the water against the hull, and all of it came together in a magnificent symphony of the sea.

I could do this forever. It was wonderful.

~ ~ ~ ~ ~ ~

22: Port Townsend Marina

Docking at the Port Townsend Boat Haven marina was a challenge.

Up until then, all of our docking experience had been at our home port of Anacortes. I think we had become overconfident.

None of us had counted on having to guide *Trixie's Destiny* into a little dual slip which was barely wider than two boats. Also, the slip was well down a line of other boats in a narrow channel, with little room to maneuver.

After seeing what was required to dock our boat, I was close to joining Charlie in the hurling event, this was so nerve-wracking.

When we docked in Anacortes it was simple. Our assigned berth was at the T-end of a dock, giving us little to worry about banging into. Unfortunately, in Port Townsend, our luck with finding an easy place to dock ran out.

Another flying analogy of sorts: Back when I was taking flying lessons, my home airport was small and there were few other airplanes around. Coming and going was a piece of cake. Seven lessons into my training, the instructor had me take the plane into a much busier airfield, this one with a control tower. There were aircraft all around us in the air as I made my approach and it scared the heck out of me. I finally had to give control over to my instructor.

Port Townsend's marina isn't as big or as busy as Anacortes, but it is narrower, and we happened to catch it at a busy time. There simply was no room for error and the situation reminded me of trying to pilot a small plane into a busy airport.

Luckily, Dawn was chosen to handle it. Charlie was still recovering from his seasickness, and neither Scott nor I had any confidence that we could do it. Getting into that berth required finding the correct slip, and then coming up alongside it in the narrow channel. After that was done, the boat needed to be turned ninety-degrees so that the aft end was facing the slip where we were then expected to back in, and with our boat having a beam—width—of nearly twenty-feet, this wide load had to be maneuvered into that narrow position without bumping into the dock on one side, or the sleek forty-four Catalina sailboat on the other side.

Even with Dawn's skills at maneuvering *Trixie's Destiny*, it took five tries.

By our third try, we had a small group of four other mariners watching us, most of them just hoping we wouldn't bump into their own boats.

By the fifth, and final, try, we had ten people on the marina watching us. Two of them with cameras going.

This was embarrassing.

One great thing about *Trixie's Destiny* was that she had three control stations. The one in the pilothouse, one up top at the fly bridge station, and one set of controls tucked away in the aft cockpit area.

It was this third set of controls that Dawn used. Given that this was our first ever attempt to back the yacht into a slip, and one immediately next to another yacht, she had chosen the aft control station as it would enable her to be right where the action was.

It was totally nerve-wracking. The first two attempts had her almost slamming our boat into the concrete side of the slip. On the third try, she came close to sideswiping the Catalina sailboat. I could see her going a bit pale and her frustration was growing.

Finally, with two other boats in the water waiting for *Trixie's Destiny* to get out of the way, Dawn pulled it off.

Scott and I jumped from the boat and onto the dock to take the ropes, while Charlie was managing the fenders. We almost looked like we knew what we were doing.

I praised Dawn mightily. Any of the three of us "macho" guys would have screwed it up so badly that our boat or the neighboring boat would have been severely damaged.

Despite our poor performance at docking, it had been done and *Trixie's Destiny* was in one piece, along with the marina and every other boat around us. I think several boat owners were relieved.

Finally, Dawn shut down the engines and we did the final tie-up. Charlie went off on wobbly legs to the marina office to check in. As he was doing this, Scott and I hooked up electric and water feeds from the marina into our boat.

This last step allowed us to have full electrical without having to run *Trixie's Destiny's* engine and systems.

Mostly, by then, we all needed a drink.

What a day. We had completed our first crossing of the Sound, entered a new port, acted as a team as we brought her in, and even Charlie had finally recovered.

Dawn had saved the day for us, and things were looking up.

Now, we had some detective work to do.

~ ~ ~ ~ ~ ~

23: Green Goose Café

"Let's review what we know, so far," Dawn said that evening, turning to her detective mode. I can see why she had been so good at it. This lady was totally focused.

After docking and checking in with the marina office we had each taken a few moments to play detective by chatting with people nearby. With this done, it was time to enjoy this charming port.

We had arrived early in the afternoon, but by the time we were ready to go out to eat and perhaps explore the town, it was nearly five. Five o'clock for folks over sixty is almost late for dinner. I used to laugh when my parents made an issue of wanting to have dinner around five or six. Not anymore, I was now one of them. When I was still working, it was common to go out for dinner with co-workers or clients, but when visiting New York or Boston, those folks didn't begin to think of having dinner before eight or nine. It was horrible. I probably shouldn't say that as the people and the restaurants were great, but it was painful to have a business dinner stretch out until ten or eleven, knowing that you had an early workday or morning flight ahead of you.

Now that was all behind me, and mostly I didn't miss it. Having friends like Scott, Charlie and Dawn, and being able to take adventures like this and explore local restaurants filled any gaps that may have resulted from my retiring.

When it came time to head out to a restaurant, we quickly realized one issue with boating: a lack of cars and limited transportation. This marina didn't have any cars for rent, not that we had thought about doing so before heading there. We had two choices: walk or catch a cab. The weather had turned nice, meaning that it was only drizzling a little, so we chose to walk.

We could have eaten on board, we certainly had dragged enough food into the galley, but we were ready to head out and find a local restaurant. Dining on *Trixie* could wait. I'm not sure why, maybe it was the stress from the day, but we wanted to be on dry land for dinner.

We checked around and were directed to the Green Goose Café, less than a ten-minute walk from the marina. Normally they were only open for breakfast and lunch. We lucked out, it was high season and they were open for dinner. Otherwise, we would have had to take a cab or put in a very long walk to find a good place to eat.

We found the restaurant to be perfect for our needs. Casual and not crowded. The number of people who appeared to be local patrons there gave us the impression that we had chosen well.

It also reminded me of McDuck's Coffee Bar, only cleaner and with more than six or seven items on the menu.

We felt right at home there in the Green Goose Café. A little later, with dinner on the table and drinks served, Dawn launched into detective mode.

"One," she started her recap, "Roger only had the boat for a few months before he was killed."

"New boat. Check," I responded as I wrote this down. It seemed a little silly, but Dawn had requested for one of us to log all of our clues and conjectures. That task was now mine.

"I don't know if the new boat thing is relevant. But, in crimes like this, there are often extraneous facts and clues. You just don't know until all of the analysis is done what clues are worthy and which ones are meaningless," Dawn advised.

"Hey, we've all seen detective shows. I know how this stuff works," Charlie complained.

"Do we know if he had a boat before *Trixie's Destiny*?" Scott asked the rest of us.

None of us had any idea about Roger's boat ownership history, so I simply jotted down "previous boats unknown."

"Next," Dawn continued her evaluation of the crime, "Roger was into some sort of import-export business. To me, this is potentially suspicious. Do any of you know what he was dealing in?"

Charlie raised his hand, as if we were back in grade school. "Ask me. Ask me," he pleaded. "I did find out, and I think it is legit. According to his widow, it turns out he was quite the importer of jewelry, mostly from South and Central America. It seems that just about every jeweler anywhere in the northwest would be likely to have his stuff on their shelves."

"Jewelry importer. South and Central America. Check," I said as I wrote this down on my list.

"So, moving on," Dawn said, sounding a bit disappointed at this tame explanation of Roger's importing activities. "Did any of you see anyone watching us or the boat when we came into port?" Dawn asked as she continued to take the lead role in the discussion.

"You've got to be kidding!" Scott laughed. "Everyone there in the marina was watching us. Seems that we have a habit of causing a crowd to gather when docking."

Dawn continued her list of facts. "Roger had two slips. One here and one in Everett. Why?"

"Also," I was able to add, "even his wife didn't know about the Port Townsend slip until after he was killed." I jotted each of these facts about slip rental onto my growing list. "Check," I added.

"So, like we said before, there is something notable about this location. We just don't know what yet," Dawn added.

"We are closer to Canada," Scott stated. "Could that be it?"

"Near Canada, check," I said, only to get a French fry thrown at me by Charlie. "What did I do?"

"You can write your little list all you want, we just don't have to hear every little bit of it repeated back immediately," Charlie clarified.

"No repeating the list out loud. Check," I chuckled as I pretended to write this down and got another set of fries pitched at me. This was good actually. My own stack of fries was running low and the resupply was welcome.

"Dufus," Scott joined in. He was clearly enjoying this. "So, back to the Canada thing, what do you think?"

"Wouldn't surprise me if the proximity to Canada has something to do with this," I responded as I paused to take a bite of my overly large burger. My wife would have frowned at my eating it as she kept me on a diet. But, damn, it tasted good. I would just have to avoid a weigh-in when I got home.

Another imagined conversation with my wife: "No dear, I ate only salads and protein. I have no idea where that extra weight came from."

"We're also close to the open sea," Dawn said.

"You're right!" Charlie said as this dawned on him. "Like when we went on the cruise. It didn't take long after going through the Strait of Juan de Fuca for us to get into the open ocean."

"You lost your dinner, if I recall!" Scott laughed, pulling up the memory of Charlie's rushing from the main dining room of the Celebrity cruise ship and out to the open deck, only to heave out his dinner in front of several onlookers.

"Gee, thanks for reminding me," Charlie responded with a pained look.

"Seasick. Check," I announced playfully as I pretended to add this to our list.

"We all talked to others today, what did we hear or learn?" Dawn was referring to the fact that we had done some poking around shortly after docking. This was, after all, a detective adventure.

"I talked with two other yacht owners," I chimed in. "Neither of them knew anything. One of them didn't even seem to know that anyone had died onboard."

"You didn't say anything about a murder, did you?" Dawn had strictly advised us to not let on about the murder. The less we would "tell," the more we would learn.

"No. The guy, two boats down knew that Roger had died, and knew it was a murder, but he saw nothing. Seems that the local police had interviewed him and he wasn't able to add much. I also talked to a couple who were just hanging around. They said they lived aboard a Lagoon Catamaran one dock over. They were the ones who didn't seem to know about anyone dying aboard the boat."

Charlie chimed in, "I got nothing. When I went to the marina office, the guy at the desk said he was sorry to hear about Roger's death, but he didn't say much more. He, I think his name was George, said it was a shame since he had just finished upgrading the boat."

"What upgrades?" Dawn asked, her attention on full alert.

"Don't know. They may have said something about upgrades to the security system or something."

"Charlie, there is no security system on the boat." Dawn said simply.

"Oh."

"Yes, oh. That, my friend, is a worthy clue. One person says they think he was upgrading the security system, yet there isn't one," Dawn said.

I now had multiple sets of eyes staring at me, waiting for me to capture this on my list. The project had grown a bit more difficult due to the grease which had dripped from my burger onto my notebook.

"I'll have another," Scott interrupted the conversation as he ordered another beer from the waiter. Then, seeing the glare Dawn was giving him, he sheepishly added, "Oh, sure, a clue. No security system. See…I was listening."

"How about you, oh Madam Detective Co-Captain?" Charlie prompted. "Did you learn anything?"

"I did have one interesting conversation," Dawn started to say.

"One interesting conversation. Check," I interrupted as I wrote this down on my list. My goal had been to obtain more fries. No such luck. I think what hit me on the forehead was a pinto bean.

Dawn continued, trying to ignore me. My guess is that she had more control of her team back when she was an actual detective than she did now; her aggravation was showing. "Anyway, I did talk to an old guy who was fishing from the pier. I had a hunch he might be around here a lot and I was right. He told me that whenever *Trixie's Destiny* was in port, another person, maybe two, would go on board but didn't stay there long."

This, we all knew, was the first really important clue. I definitely wrote this down.

"Did he give any details?" Scott asked.

"No, unfortunately," she responded as she took a sip of her white wine. "He didn't think of it as unusual, so he didn't pay much attention."

I took the last available bite of my burger. One of the best I'd had in years. I started to mumble out a question over my mouthful, but Charlie beat me to it.

"So, what now?"

"Now, my friends," Dawn announced, "we take a nice stroll back to the boat, get a good night's sleep, and tomorrow a couple of us can go to the police station and see if we can find out anything more."

~ ~ ~ ~ ~ ~

24: First Night Onboard

Charlie snores.

I know this because his cabin is next to mine and the insulation in the thin walls didn't do near enough to kill the sound.

Now I know what my wife had to put up with for so many years. It wasn't until I lost weight, a result of the diet she had me on, that I had stopped snoring. The snoring thing was a side benefit but it definitely made her happier and I was sleeping better. Charlie, it seems, could benefit from the same plan.

Mid-way through our first night onboard, I was seriously envying Dawn. She had chosen wisely when she selected the crew area in the aft of the boat as her cabin and place to sleep.

It wasn't just Charlie's snoring which kept me awake, although it was the primary cause. It was also the sounds of the boat at night, water lapping against the side, the creaking of the fenders against the dock, and the varied movements as we gently bobbled about.

The idealistic notion of spending nights on a yacht was quickly fading. I still wanted to do it, and I wanted to take the long trips, but this one night had taught me some of the realities of living on a boat.

Now, if we could just find a way to muffle Captain Charlie's snoring.

Finally, the long night was over, and I went up to the galley to get a cup of coffee. Having coffee before my morning shower, and while listening to the news, was one of the great habits I had developed since retiring. Now, I was hoping to carry this habit to *Trixie*. I even put on sweatpants and a sweatshirt for the occasion.

Dawn was already there, and it was the first time I had seen her without makeup and her day clothes. Like me, she was just wearing sweats. It was a nice change to see her so relaxed. We used the Keurig for coffee, which was very convenient and allowed for a variety of coffee preferences. Each coffee was poured into a separate mug with a picture of the Grand Banks Yachts logo on it. This pleasant task complete, we sat down at the dining table.

"How'd you sleep?" she asked, just making idle conversation.

"It may take some getting used to," I said simply, not wanting to rip into Charlie and his snoring.

"Not me," she answered and then sipped her coffee. "I was out immediately. That berth is a little small, but I'm not all that big, so it worked just fine. Cozy."

We sat there sipping coffee for a bit longer, enjoying the early morning there in the marina. The sun was rising and we could see we were likely to have a nice day ahead of us.

"Still up for long trips?" she asked as we looked out from the pilothouse to watch two men board a small boat with fishing gear at the ready.

"Definitely. Like I said, it will take some adjustments, but I want to do this. I especially like the idea of a trip up through the inside passage to Alaska. I remember when our cruise ship pulled into Ketchikan and I saw a few yachts there. Then, later, we went up the fjord to see the glacier and we passed another yacht similar to *Trixie's Destiny*. I really envied those people, and I want to have that same experience."

"Even if there may be bad guys out there who are looking for something on this boat?"

"Hey, that's why we have you and Scott on this team. Your jobs are to keep us safe, Charlie's is to drive the boat…if he can keep from puking, and my role is to sit back and watch it all unfold."

"Check!" she mocked my checklist mantra from the evening before.

We finished our coffees and each drifted down to our respective areas. For me, it was a simple matter of popping down the stairs from the galley to the cabins below. For Dawn, she had to go outside and make her way to the separate external door that then led down to the crew quarters and engine room.

Soon, I was working on my first shower onboard the yacht. I only banged my elbows thirty or forty times in the process. That head and the little shower are small! Back when we had taken the cruise, I had thought the shower in our concierge-level cabin was small. It now seemed gargantuan compared to this.

Twenty minutes later, I was dressed, shaved and ready to face the world. My cabin was plenty big for me and for my garb; it would just take a while to get used to the small head. Still, I had a cabin to myself, as we all did, and that was pretty good. The one thing I missed was a window where I could see out. On the cruise ship, each of our cabins had balconies with sliding glass doors. On this boat, there was only a little porthole and the minimal light it let in did little to reduce the closed-in feeling.

We had a great breakfast onboard. None of us had even discussed roles for cooking and cleaning, it just happened, and reasonably well. Scott, it turns out, makes an incredible bacon-mushroom-cheese-tomato omelet. I was happy to stand aside and let him take command of the galley to produce his masterpiece. I worked on setting up the table and dishware and functioning as sous chef to Scott when he needed it. Charlie and Dawn agreed to take on the post-breakfast cleaning duty.

Scott was our new hero. We had no previous inkling of his culinary skills. I think he had kept it that way on purpose. Now, though, if this one breakfast was a sign of things to come, we had some great meals ahead of us.

During breakfast, we compared notes on our sleeping experiences from the night before. I was the only one who had a restless night. Again, I said nothing about Charlie's snoring, and neither did Scott. So, it seems that I was the only one bothered by it. I had a solution in mind...go buy earplugs at the first opportunity.

"Scott and I are going to the police station. I was able to set up an appointment with Sam Lane, the detective there who ran the casefile on Roger," Dawn announced and added that she and Scott would be taking a short cab ride to get to the police station that was about one mile away. She had wanted to keep the conversation cop-to-cop, which made sense, but it forced Charlie and me to come up with activities on our own.

We decided to just hang around the marina for the few hours before we left. Our current plans were to pull out from the marina around noon, which would get us back into Anacortes around three or so.

Another interesting thing about yachting. You didn't have to factor traffic into your timing as you did when driving into or out of a city. I really loved that aspect of it. Just leave when you feel like it and head on out, with no worry of getting stuck in traffic.

We were also supposed to play detective some more, but I had no clue what to "detect" at this point.

~ ~ ~ ~ ~ ~

25: Leaving Port Townsend

"He had been shot with a small caliber pistol," Dawn reported to us later, as we were heading away from Port Townsend. She and Scott had spent over an hour with Detective Lane and exchanged every bit of information they had. For the Port Townsend detective, this was still an open case and he was anxious to obtain any intelligence he could. For Dawn and Scott, this was a matter of curiosity and perhaps even self-preservation. We needed to keep from having anyone else come in search of "it," and do so with potentially harmful consequences to one or more of our little group.

Detective Lane was extremely interested when Dawn described how Viktor had snuck aboard, threatened me, and been in search of some unknown object. The detective vowed to get in touch with the Coast Guard and seek out Viktor to interview him.

I learned all of this while piloting the yacht. For the second leg of our return journey, I was at the helm, sitting on the top deck as Dawn and Scott relayed their findings.

Charlie had taken the first leg, that of getting us out of the marina and into the bay. I prayed that Charlie would be able to do so without damaging something. He did. It was helpful that the sailboat, which had been sharing the double slip, was gone, giving us more maneuvering room. Finally, and with three very anxious co-captains watching his every move, we made it out of the marina and did so with only one angry boater yelling at us. Once again, Charlie had fouled up a right-of-way.

With this major achievement accomplished, and Port Townsend fully in our rear view, Charlie handed the controls over to me. He had wanted to go down to the head. My guess was, he had scared the crap out of himself during the process of exiting the marina and needed to go to the head just to settle his nerves.

I loved driving this beautiful boat, and it was a gorgeous day. We also had minimal boating traffic to concern ourselves with. A Washington State Ferry passed a few hundred yards ahead of us, but that was the only boat I had to watch out for just then.

"They found the bullet; it was still in the body. Not uncommon for a small caliber. I doubt that Roger died immediately. The detective thought the same thing."

"Makes you wonder why he was shot while on the john and why, if he didn't die immediately, he stayed where he was," Charlie asked our two police friends. He had returned from below and was now enjoying simply sitting there on the top deck with the rest of us as I maneuvered the boat along.

"My conjecture is the bad guy, or guys, kept him there and didn't let him leave. I would also guess that they were grilling him about where 'it' was the whole time he was dying," Scott added.

"That's a lot of conjecture," I responded while giving the rest of my attention to two kayakers who were off to port about fifty yards away. I slowed down to reduce the wake as a small help to them.

The four of us sat there on the fly bridge as we enjoyed the movements of the boat and the feel of the sea. Luckily, Charlie was not showing signs of seasickness. I think he was learning his lesson. No McBeignets, hamburgers, hot dogs, or anything greasy for lunch. He had satisfied himself with a simple cheese sandwich and a Ginger Ale when we had prepared our lunch while still in the marina. He was starting to learn and understand some of the cause-and-effect as it related to his food choices on board.

"Did you two learn anything more?" Dawn asked Charlie who was sitting beside me at the helm.

"I learned that I was wrong about Roger upgrading the security system. Or, at least, maybe I was. They changed their story a bit and now say that they simply knew that

Roger was doing some upgrades but had no idea what it was."

"We also got the name of the outfit that was doing the upgrades: Upper Puget Marine Systems," I relayed the company name to the others.

"You should have gone to visit them. We could have waited," Dawn said with a bit of disappointment in us.

"No such company," I replied. "We would have checked them out if we could have, but they don't exist."

"Really," Charlie added. "We checked online, asked the people in the marina office and even checked the local business directory. No such company."

"Oh, well, thanks for looking into it," Dawn responded. "Do you think the marina office people gave you false information?"

"Didn't seem that way to me," Charlie responded for the two of us. "But, I'm not the detective."

"Could it be that the people from that phony company used it as a ruse to obtain permission to go onto *Trixie* and then kill Roger?" Scott asked.

This, to me, sounded totally plausible. Seeing Dawn ponder this, told me that she thought so as well.

"What about you and Scott?" I asked, I had to speak up to be heard as I had ramped up our speed to fifteen knots, which caused the wind noise to increase, making it harder to talk.

"Our Port Townsend detective friend didn't have much more to add. He even checked out the video footage from the few cameras there at the marina and he had nothing to report," Dawn said, her voice louder so she could be heard.

"Didn't help that the camera directed to our part of the marina wasn't working, so there was no footage to view," Scott added derisively. "Nothing suspicious there, of course."

I took a moment to check the navigational bearings and adjusted the direction two degrees to starboard. I wanted to stay in calmer waters. Plus, this would bring us closer in to Whidbey Island, where we would have more scenery to view as we cruised along.

Charlie added some more information, gleaned from the minimal detective work he and I had done earlier. "We chatted with a guy in the trawler four boats down from where our slip was. Seems that the owner of the sailboat berthed next to *Trixie* and Roger were BFFs. According to Tim, the trawler guy, the owner of the sailboat and Roger were seen moving stuff from boat-to-boat whenever they were both in port."

"That could be who the old fisherman saw. Remember, he had said something about one or two people going onto *Trixie's Destiny* whenever Roger was in port," Dawn summarized.

"We definitely need to learn more about that sailboat," Scott stated. "Did either of you get info on it?"

Charlie gave a broad smile. "I got photos of it. Took them when Dawn almost crashed into it when we were docking. One picture has the name of the boat clear as day. No people on board in the picture, though," Charlie plainly enjoyed relaying how Dawn had come close to hitting the neighboring boat. It was as if he needed to prove he wasn't the only one whose boating skills were a bit flawed.

I wasn't about to summarize the difference in flaw count between Dawn and Charlie. It was best to leave that one alone.

"Her name, uh, the sailboat that had been docked next to us, was named the *Smooth Seas*, and she was out of Victoria, British Columbia."

"Good going, Charlie," Dawn responded, ignoring Charlie's jibes. "That same boat was gone by the time we got back from dinner last night, wasn't it?" she added.

"Yep," Charlie responded, simply.

"We will definitely be checking that sailboat out," Scott said. "Good going, Charlie."

I could see Charlie beaming from this compliment.

"Kinda interesting how the *Smooth Seas* was gone right after we arrived in port," Charlie said what we had all been thinking.

Did our arrival in Port Townsend cause the owner of the *Smooth Seas* to skedaddle out of there?

~ ~ ~ ~ ~ ~

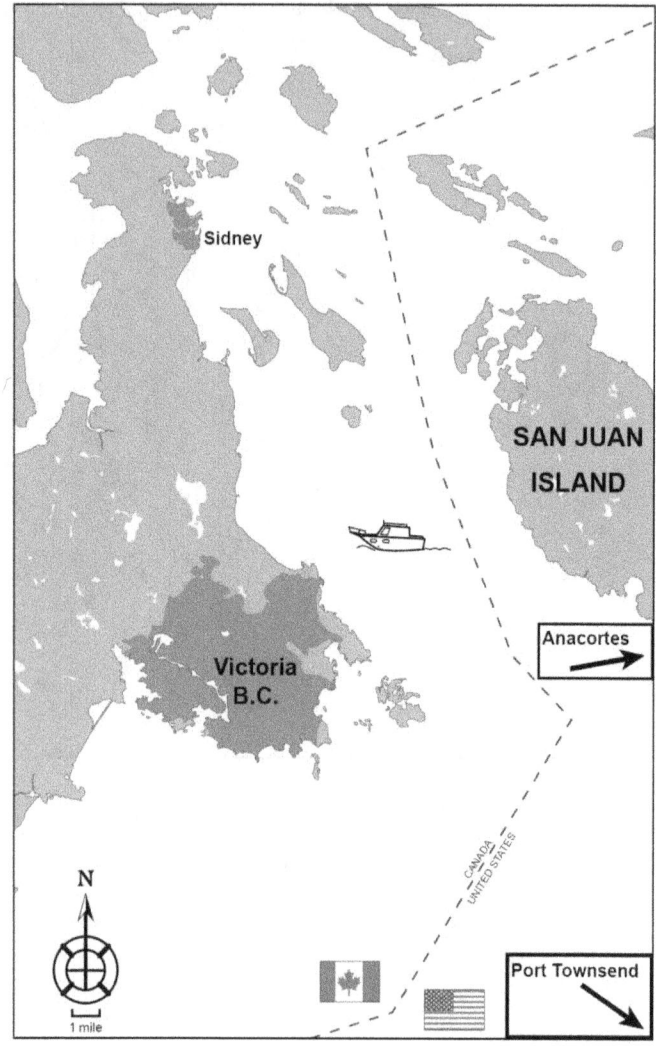

VICTORIA B.C. AREA

Sidney

SAN JUAN
ISLAND

Anacortes

Victoria
B.C.

CANADA
UNITED STATES

N

Port Townsend

1 mile

26: High Tea

Three days after returning to Anacortes, Francine and I took a trip with our daughter, Emily, her husband Edward, an insurance agent with his own office in Anacortes, and our granddaughter Emma.

We were headed to Victoria, British Columbia.

Anacortes is perfectly positioned for this. All we had to do was take our car a few minutes from our home to the ferry dock, drive onto the magnificent old Washington State ferry, and then spend a wonderful few hours up on deck as we weaved our way through the San Juans on the way to Sidney, the ferry stop on Vancouver Island. After going through a quick customs check, it was just a short distance to the small city of Victoria.

This was our first family outing since Francine and I had moved out west from Ohio, and it was a great way to reconnect with them. I had spent hours going through *Trip Advisor* and other online sites and, as a result, had several fun activities planned.

First, we checked into the Fairmont Empress Hotel, facing the lively Inner Harbour. That splendid old Canadian Pacific hotel is a true classic, and one of our first activities was to indulge in an English "High Tea." Francine was totally looking forward to this and wanted for our daughter and granddaughter to sit in on one. We had done high tea when touring England and had enjoyed it. Now, it was time to share the experience.

As expected, the tea event was enjoyed by everyone in our group except for Edward, my son-in-law. He is a sports nut and having to sit through a formal tea for over an hour, while a variety of games on TV were going unwatched, was excruciating for him.

I had a surprise for Edward though. We had tickets to a cricket game the next day at Beacon Hill Park to watch Victoria United play a team from Vancouver. During high tea was not the time to tell him, so I just let him fidget. Francine and I had watched a cricket game with friends while touring Australia, and I didn't understand a lick of it. It would be interesting to see if sports-obsessed Edward would be able to figure it out.

To fill in the time while Francine, Emily, Emma and I enjoyed our tea and scones, Edward found a local Victoria, BC paper to read.

I really didn't like him doing that, but if this was going to keep him from complaining while the rest of us enjoyed the occasion, then so be it.

Then I saw a headline just below the fold on the first page of the paper. Edward's attention was on the sports section, he had placed the other sections on the table between us. When I looked down, I saw the bold letters, "*Local Gem Merchant Dies While Sailing.*"

For some reason, that article really caught my attention. Apologizing to Francine, I picked up the front section of the paper from the table and quickly scanned the article. Two words jumped off of the page at me...*Smooth Seas.* This was the name of the boat parked next to *Trixie's Destiny* when we visited Port Townsend. I also recalled how the name on the stern of that boat had identified it as being from Victoria.

According to the article, the death appeared to be a result of suicide, although the cause was not certain. He didn't have a wife, but his daughter lived in Vancouver and details were being held until she had been notified. I read on and learned that the boat had been found drifting outside of Port Angeles, a Washington State town across from Victoria. A fishing boat had come across it and two of the crew boarded the sailboat after no one responded to their hail.

I had to pass this information on to Dawn or Scott. This might be important. Then, it hit me that this guy, Herbert Langton, was a major dealer of gems. Roger Amund had been an importer of gems and such, and he had died while onboard *Trixie*.

This was simply too close in details to be a coincidence.

Somehow, the very recent death of Herbert Langton and Roger were related. They had to be. Both men were major distributors of jewelry. They each had sizeable boats. They had adjoining slips in Port Townsend. They had been seen passing "stuff" between them when both boats were in port. And, most importantly, they were both now dead and had died while on their boats.

I pulled out my cellphone and worked up a quick email which I sent to Dawn and Scott and detailed what I had read, I also told them were they could find the article online.

Less than five minutes later, I received a response from Dawn expressing her amazement and concern at this. She also said that she passed the information on to Detective Lane at Port Townsend. My duty done, I tried to turn my attention back to the enjoyable high tea and the excellent service the hotel staff provided.

Focusing on tea and not on the deaths of two gem and jewelry importers wasn't exactly easy.

Francine had been curious as to what I was up to when I had been studying the newspaper article so closely instead of focusing on our high tea, and then sending off the message as I did. I just couldn't clue her into what was going on. She would worry too much. So, I gave her a half-truth and told her how the boat *Smooth Seas* had been in Port Townsend when we were, and now the owner had died from an apparent suicide.

She asked if we had met the man and I was able to tell her that we hadn't. I had thought I had seen him on board *Smooth Seas* when we first docked, and had darn near sideswiped his boat, but wasn't sure.

Luckily, this set off no alarm bells with my wife. So, we finished our meal, and I turned my attention away from the article and the disturbing news.

With our event at the Empress Hotel done, it was time to have some fun, and our entertainment went by the name of Henrietta the Hippo. Really. In looking for activities that I thought all of us, spanning three generations, could enjoy together, I came upon the hippo tours. They are amphibious busses which tour both on land and in the water. Ours just happened to be named Henrietta.

It was fantastic! The best part, and the part that our granddaughter loved the most, was when the tour bus turned away from the land-based portion of the tour and headed down a concrete ramp to splash into the water.

Water flew up alongside Henrietta the Hippo and our open windows, causing Emma to squeal in delight.

Once in the water, we went near a huge cruise ship which towered over us, then we motored around a point of land and into the Inner Harbour where we were able to watch the many water taxis dart to-and-fro around us.

After this, it was time to walk the area around the Inner Harbour and take in the sights. Our next two days were planned fully with the cricket game and a tour to the expansive Butchart Gardens.

If it just weren't for that bit about the sailboat *Smooth Seas* and the odd death of its owner Herbert Langton, everything would have been great.

~ ~ ~ ~ ~ ~

27: Inspector Gibson

We heard back almost immediately from the detective in Port Townsend. After receiving the information from Dawn, he contacted the Canadian Coast Guard detachment in Victoria. It turns out that the newspaper didn't exactly have it right about it being a suicide.

Put another way, Herbert Langton had been murdered, plain and simple. The news people simply had been told that Mr. Langton was found dead; somehow, the press in Victoria turned that into suicide. The Canadian Coast Guard and the Victoria, BC, officials who had taken on the case saw no reason to correct them on this. They could now investigate the murder without having members of the press poking around in their work.

Detective Lane from Port Townsend and Inspector Gibson from Victoria were interested in learning everything they could from each of us, while at the same time they both wanted for us to stay far away from anything that felt like detective work.

Fine with me, although I think Dawn was a bit disappointed.

Soon, we were on a video conference via Dawn's iPad with the detective and the inspector, telling them everything we knew. Their questions went on and on and it was almost as if we were now the suspects in the murder.

Especially Charlie. He really seemed to be the center of their queries. It didn't help that he had obtained the boat so soon after Roger's death, and so cheaply...if you can call nearly three million dollars cheap. I think this scared Charlie, once he tuned into their line of questioning.

Then it totally freaked him out. After the video call, Inspector Gibson was on the ferry the next morning to come and see us, while Detective Lane was doing the same from his direction.

A chat with the police officials over an iPad was one thing. Having both an inspector and a detective coming to see us, representing two different countries, was way more than Charlie was prepared to handle.

They were ostensibly coming to tour *Trixie's Destiny*, but Charlie took this as a sign that he should try to figure out what size orange prison jumpsuit he should order.

When they arrived the next morning, Charlie tried to head them off by first meeting them in the marina parking lot and edging them toward McDuck's Coffee Bar where he had a plate of warm McBeignets waiting and ready. They would have nothing of this. The detective and the inspector wanted to see our yacht and they wanted to question us further.

Charlie just wanted to cry.

Seeing the rest of us standing on the dock with our caps proudly announcing our Co-Captain status caused them to pause. The inspector from Victoria evaluated each of us, looking at our caps and then at our faces, as if he was striving to determine if we were serious or perhaps attempting to mess with him. In the end, he just chuckled and turned to face our boat.

Soon, they were onboard *Trixie's Destiny* as Charlie led them on a tour while Scott, Dawn and I sat quietly in the main salon. The detectives paid us little interest. It was the boat they were mostly interested in. Maybe Charlie as well, but their attentions were on the boat.

Their inspection seemed thorough, with the two men poking their heads into numerous nooks and crannies as they went from one part of our boat to another. Bottom-line, they really didn't know what they were looking for so, after a while, they quit. In the end, the inspector simply praised us for keeping a well-maintained boat.

We all liked hearing that.

Just as we were all relaxing from the compliments, the inspector found a small notebook in the galley. It was in a small drawer none of us had ever opened as it was down low and out of the way. The notebook was mostly just a list of names, numbers and email addresses.

The other dead guy, Herbert Langton, was on that list. So were names from individuals in a half dozen South American countries.

Charlie was close to throwing up.

I wasn't exactly happy just then either. What did the presence of this notebook with Herbert Langton's contact info in it mean?

It was a good thing that we had told Detective Lane earlier that Herbert Langton and Roger Amund had known each other and had been seen together at the Port Townsend marina more than once. Otherwise, this might have looked very suspicious.

Inspector Gibson placed the notebook in an evidence bag and just gave Charlie an appraising look, and then did the same with us.

Charlie might have been nervous. Dawn was getting pissed. She had pulled the same tactics on others while investigating cases. Now she was on the receiving end of it and she didn't like being in this situation one bit.

It was odd how I could feel so guilty while knowing full well that I wasn't. And, if Charlie's expression and body language meant anything, I'm sure he believed he was about to spend the rest of his days in either a Canadian or a U.S. prison.

I wonder which one would be better.

Finally, the inspection was done. It had taken a little over an hour. Their next step was to go visit with Viktor Jairo, the individual who had snuck onto *Trixie's Destiny* during our family day cruise, and who was now awaiting trial while being held in a brig at the Whidbey Island Naval Air Station. It seems that our local Coast Guard regularly used the facilities on that small navy base to house their detainees. Now, this was where Detective Lane and Inspector Gibson would be heading.

After that, the inspector wanted to interview Amanda Amund. We provided her contact information, which relieved Charlie as it seemed to take the pressure off him.

In the end, they praised us for being so helpful and the inspector, switching to boating, talked with us about our desire to take *Trixie's Destiny* up to Alaska. He had done this twice before, on boats much smaller than ours, and he had a lot of good information to pass on. I found myself writing down details on a half-dozen inlets and islands we could explore.

I had expected that either the detective or the inspector would tell us to stay in town, but they didn't. They simply made sure that we had each other's contact information and seemed to have no problem with our plans to head north.

The Inspector did warn us to keep alert. Something was amiss and two people had already died. I could see that having two retired police officers, Scott and Dawn, as fellow co-captains greatly helped in Inspector Gibson's eyes.

Once they were gone, Charlie threw up.

This time he didn't quite make it to the side of the boat to spew forth.

It's his yacht, let him clean it up.

~ ~ ~ ~ ~ ~

28: Armed to the Gills

Before Inspector Gibson departed, he passed on several details of Langton's death. I think this was done simply as a professional courtesy to Dawn and Scott. Whatever the motive, the information was disturbing.

Langton had died by a small caliber pistol, just like Roger Amund, and it had looked a bit like Roger's death in that Langton was left to die. It wasn't quick. He had been found dead in the small forward cabin, with the cabin door blocked from outside to keep him trapped. The hatch, which normally would have allowed him to escape from the cabin's ceiling into the bow area, had also been blocked. Langton had little choice but to die a slow death as he bled out from his wounds.

About the only difference between the two murders was that Langton's boat had been thoroughly ripped apart, while *Trixie's Destiny* had only select areas disturbed with stuff strewn about. As with *Trixie*, it was clear that the bad guys had been looking for something.

With any luck, they had found it and any possible threat to us was past.

Dawn didn't believe this for a minute. She had worked too many cases over the years and resolution was often far from simple. In her mind, the bad guy was still out there looking for something and we were all at risk.

So, with Dawn's prompting, and Scott's built-in paranoia, resulting from years of working as a police officer, *Trixie's Destiny* soon had a full armory on board. I hated that!

With the deaths of the two men, Scott and Dawn were extremely concerned that someone might come after one of us. Given that the two other fatalities had occurred while they were on their boats, Scott was convinced that this was where a problem would arise. If a problem arose.

I couldn't count all of the weapons we had, but we had a boatload of them... excuse the expression. Even automatic weapons. They were now discretely tucked away in various places throughout the yacht. There were multiple reasons for this. One of them was that we would be crossing into Canada, and the Canadian Firearms Act had some major restrictions on weapons, especially hidden and automatic weapons. In the U.S. we probably could have had a gun turret on top of the boat, and no one would have said anything.

Given our location in Anacortes, and planned travels, we would be crossing the border between the two countries multiple times. The solution was simple. Hide the weapons and hide them well.

Theoretically no one, bad guys or even the Coast Guard, would ever know they were there they were so well hidden. They were also wrapped well to prevent the sea air from getting to them. Hiding the weapons throughout the boat had been Dawn's idea. Her rationalization was that we had to be ready for problems anywhere and everywhere on board.

Once we were done turning *Trixie's Destiny* into a miniature battleship, we went through numerous drills as to where the weapons were. Dawn wanted for us to know how to get to a weapon in an instant, from anywhere onboard. By the end of that day's training, I knew which couches to reach up and under for a rifle. Which compartments in the cockpit had weapons stored, and on the list went.

Then it was time for Charlie and me to take firearms training. Bottom-line, I am much better at making Power Point presentations than I will ever be at shooting cardboard cutout figures. Just ask everyone at the indoor firing range. Some of them may have even ducked for cover.

The only good thing about my performance with weapons was that Captain Charlie made me look good.

After our shooting range experience and with us all familiar with the locations of every weapon, Scott had us all go through onboard "bad guy drills" as he came up with different scenarios. In one case, he had Charlie be the bad guy, holding Dawn hostage. Scott and I were then to resolve the situation. I quietly retrieved a pistol from a forward locker and crept up on Charlie as he held an unloaded weapon, pretending to threaten Dawn. Scott did the same from the starboard side, with me doing my best ninja-stealth act to surprise Charlie from the port side.

I died.

It reminded me of the military maneuvers I did way back in ROTC when I was in college. I was "killed" multiple times during those drills. Just as I was "killed" during our first drills on board. The really bad part was, not only did I get myself "killed" by the enemy—in this case the pretend Viet Cong—I managed to get my squad killed as well.

I earned very few merits during those ROTC training sessions.

Then, after working with Scott again and again, something clicked. I don't know what exactly or why, but I soon found that I was able to sneak up—even on Dawn—and "take her out" with my weapons. We didn't shoot anything, of course, I simply yelled out "bang," but it was realistic enough.

Finally, Scott and Dawn announced that I wasn't half-bad, and Charlie was less likely to kill himself accidentally than he had first been. For us, this was a shining endorsement.

This whole thing with the weapons was something else I held back from my wife. I hated doing it, but had I told her how we were now armed to the gills and I was learning how to shoot at, well, people, she would have totally freaked.

So, with *Trixie* now armed and the four of us more or less trained in how to handle an armed bad guy, we were ready for our first big adventure.

I had just never planned on doing this with AK47s at the ready.

~ ~ ~ ~ ~ ~

29: Final Plans and Details

Our big adventure started in early July. Three weeks after my jaunt over to Victoria with my family, and a week after Charlie and I had completed our arms training.

The plan had first been to go to Juneau and back. If a cruise ship could do it, we certainly could. Then, sanity prevailed. The trip to Juneau was about nine hundred miles, as the seagull flies, each way. Not much, in theory, but for novice boaters, and for a trip into a truly rugged area with little help available if something were to go wrong, it was too much.

So, we cut our first big adventure down. Ketchikan, Alaska was our new goal. It was still about six hundred "normal" miles, or five hundred plus nautical miles, away and a trip to be proud of.

By completing this journey, we would be able to say we had boated up to Alaska, even if we had only made it a very short way into that state.

And, if we so chose, we could easily turn around at any time. Prince Rupert, BC, for example would make a fine destination and one we could be proud of reaching.

Common sense said that even this shortened voyage was not a good idea. We were simply too new at this. More than one of the seasoned boat captains around the marina in Anacortes advised us against it, stating that we should simply hang around the Puget Sound for a few seasons before attempting a trip northward.

Screw that. We wanted to do it.

We read and reread manuals, route guides and boating blogs. Each of us took on a different geographical area to study so that we would be "local experts." That worked pretty well. My sector of expertise was from Anacortes up to Campbell River on Vancouver Island. The others each took sectors of a similar length with some overlap built in.

It was fun to go over findings and maps to discuss possible stops and detours with each other as we sat in Mac's sipping our Duzy-size coffees while gorging on McBeignets.

Poor Mac. His business would be taking a nosedive with us gone.

One huge difference between taking a cruise and taking a boating trip soon became obvious as we talked over the upcoming trip. When cruising, the ship often moved along at night while you slept, and then during the day you were in port to play and explore. With yachting, the opposite was about to occur. We didn't dare plan on traveling at night. All travel was to happen during the day, and then we would sleep while in port or tied up in a cove or inlet somewhere.

While this route planning was taking place, we had mechanics come on to *Trixie's Destiny* to check out the engine, stabilizers, propellers, thrusters, pumps, holding tanks, lines, fenders, navigation, radar, radio and numerous other items of equipment. Then, based on their guidance, we stocked up on spare parts, those most likely to need replacing, such as extra propellers and an extra anchor. The storage areas in the engine room were crammed full.

Charlie had also ordered up extra uniforms and extra co-captain's caps to add to the oversupply we already had.

So, the boat was ready. We were ready, now we only had to say our goodbyes and head on out.

The goal was to take about one week to get to Ketchikan and our pace would be around one hundred miles a day. *Trixie* could get us there faster, but that wasn't what we wanted. The best and most economical cruise speed was around fourteen or fifteen miles per hour, twelve knots. So, this is what we would do.

At that rate, and assuming a route diversion or two each day, we would be in the water around seven hours a day to maintain our hundred-miles-daily objective. Not a lot of time, but far more than we had experienced to date.

The return voyage promised to be very different and a lot of fun. We would have guests on board with us.

Charlie had offered to spring for a charter flight from the county airport near Anacortes up to Ketchikan, or Prince Rupert should our plans change. Chartering a plane like this was one of the advantages of having loads of money, as Charlie did. I certainly couldn't afford it on my retirement check.

My wife, Scott's wife, and Dawn's new special friend, Tony Drew, were going to take that private flight up to Ketchikan to join us. They would then be aboard *Trixie's Destiny* for the return voyage.

I was really looking forward to the return leg. The boat might be a bit crowded, but it would be fun, and we would be able to show off some of the sights and places we hoped to discover on our way up.

"What about you?" Dawn asked Charlie as we sat in McDuck's Coffee Bar two days before our planned departure. "It doesn't seem right that the rest of us will have someone with us for the return trip and you won't."

Charlie just looked sheepish and didn't respond.

"You have someone, don't you?" Dawn exclaimed, seeing the look on our friend's face. "Tell us more, fella."

Scott and I put on the chant of "Charlie. Charlie. Charlie," until he finally relented.

"I kinda met someone," Charlie admitted, and boy was he blushing.

"And, we're just now finding this out!" Dawn said flabbergasted. "Really, Charlie, what gives?"

"I was embarrassed to say anything. You three can be such shits and all."

I had to laugh. Charlie was probably right. Had he told us about a new love, we wouldn't have given him a moment of peace. Kind of like we were doing just then.

"Tell all, Charlie!" Dawn commanded.

"Her name is Janet," he said simply.

"Oh, so she has a name at least. That would imply that she is living and human and all," Scott teased. "She is human, right?"

"Like I said, you all can be shits," Charlie responded, but I could see a note of pride in him just then.

Dawn looked at Scott and me. "Guys shut up for a moment and let Captain Charlie tell us all about it. Then, if you are nice, I will let you each have another McBeignet."

"I accept that deal," Scott said for the two of us.

Charlie looked at each of us, and seeing that we were inclined to play nice, went on to describe how Janet was a realtor he had met and that she was about five years younger than him. They had met while shopping for groceries.

"Oh, there are so many jokes about that grocery thing, please, pretty please, let me say some of them!" Scott chuckled. "Ouch!" he quickly added as Dawn kicked at him under the table.

Funny thing was, I had no clue as to what Scott was referring to. I smiled as if I knew what all of those grocery-dating jokes might be, not wanting to look dumb. I couldn't come up with a one myself. Apparently, Scott had several jokes in mind. I would have to ask him about them one day.

Maybe not. I've heard his joke repertoire, and there wasn't one I would want to repeat. Not in mixed company, anyway.

Charlie pulled out his cellphone and showed us a picture of her. I must admit, Charlie had done well. Looking back at us from that portrait was an attractive, smiling, mature woman with intelligent eyes. She had short gray hair and appeared to be a little heavy, like Charlie.

Bottom-line, Charlie and Janet had been dating for nearly three weeks and the rest of us had been clueless about it. Now, she was to be the fourth guest for our return voyage from Ketchikan on *Trixie's Destiny*.

A thought occurred to me and I couldn't hold back. "Charlie, you will have a new lady friend with you and those walls between our cabins are awfully thin," I stared at him, willing him to understand my meaning without having to say anything. "Get my drift?"

He gave me a blank look.

"I can hear you snore and fart through those walls, Charlie!" I tried to clarify.

"Oh. She doesn't snore," Charlie responded simply.

Scott laughed, and Charlie still looked puzzled.

"Can you really hear me snore through the cabin walls?"

I just looked at him. "Charlie, my loveable captain and friend, that was not my point."

Dawn, shaking her head in dismay, shoved a McBeignet into my mouth and then did the same with Charlie.

Not a bad way to end an otherwise futile discussion.

~ ~ ~ ~ ~ ~

30: Crossing to Nanaimo

The first leg of our grand journey was a short one; we were headed to Point Roberts simply because we wanted to say we had been there. The plan was to stop at the marina in Point Roberts, go visit a historical marker, maybe get lunch and then head out to our final destination for the day, Nanaimo, British Columbia. A total of eighty-plus "normal" miles for our first day.

None of us were attuned to speaking in nautical measurements. Knots. Nautical Miles, and such. It sounded pretentious. So, we resorted to speaking in normal distance and speed terms.

I was the one who had requested the first short stop. There is a geographic oddity about this place which was just too good to pass up. Point Roberts, simply said, is in the wrong country. The small, five square mile spit of land, is physically attached to Canada, and is basically a suburb of the city of Vancouver. But, with history's various twists and turns, this one little area ended up as part of the U.S.

To get there by car from the U.S. meant that you must first head north on I-5 into Canada, go through a potentially long customs process, turn west for a while, and then back south to go back into Point Roberts. Oh, and go through customs again.

We chose, instead, to go by boat; so, no customs at all as we would never have left the country. The area of land at Point Roberts may be small, but that marina is huge. Probably even larger than any of the marinas around Anacortes.

This was only our third marina to visit, but we handled it like pros this time. A temporary slip was reserved in advance, we had checked out the marina map so we would know where to dock, and even looked at the tidal charts. We radioed the marina office as we arrived, and they had an attendant there to take the lines we tossed out to him. Within a few minutes, we were secured.

It took almost three hours to get to Point Roberts from Anacortes, and we spent less than two hours there. Other than the historical marker, there wasn't anything to see.

We had done it. We had visited this misplaced part of the U.S. Now we were ready to really start our trip and head northwest to Nanaimo.

With many hours and days of boating ahead of us, we decided to divide into two teams. One team, Scott and I, would pilot the boat, watch for other boats and obstacles, and just handle any other issue that might arise. While we managed *Trixie's Destiny*, the other team, Dawn and Charlie, would play passenger as they rested, ate or watched the satellite TV.

In theory this would work well. In practice, we all seemed to be around each other at the helm. Only when Scott had gone down to the galley to get sandwiches, did we have any separation of our foursome.

Another thing about yachting became apparent. We would spend almost zero time in our cabins during the day. Other than to change or go to the head, the below decks areas remained largely abandoned as we cruised along.

There were many reasons for this; chief among them was that it was dark and closed-in down there. The Grand Banks Aleutian yachts are beautifully appointed, but with few windows in the lower deck, it is gloomy. Okay for sleeping, but not much more.

We spent the afternoon of our first day in an uneventful cruise from Point Roberts across the Strait of Georgia, finding our way over the top of Gabriola Island, a long and narrow island, and finally to the large Townsite Marina in Nanaimo where we had a reserved slip for the night.

The scenery across the strait and all during the last forty-five miles of our trip had been absolutely wonderful. During those three and a half hours, we relaxed, talked about the exciting places we were going to visit, and we even passed by a large Princess Cruise ship which was probably on its way from Vancouver to points south.

Several folks on the cruise ship waved at us, with many taking photos of *Trixie's Destiny*. We, in turn, did the same. We probably took as many pictures of that huge white ship as they did of us.

This was heaven.

That night, after docking in Nanaimo, checking in with Canadian customs and securing the boat to our slip, we had a great pizza dinner at a local pub. Later, while strolling along a walkway next to the marina, I called Francine and brought her up to date on our events so far.

She was excited about the prospect of the upcoming chartered flight to Ketchikan in several days and had held several conversations with Sally, Scott's wife, about the trip. When I told her about Charlie's new lady friend, Janet, my wife was delighted.

Then, Francine asked how many suitcases she could bring. She didn't like my answer. Zero. There really wasn't room, especially given that I had the smallest of the three main cabins. She could bring on a soft-sided duffel bag, as I had done, but not much more than that.

I could hear her disappointment over the phone and knew that she would likely ignore my advice. With her inclination to pack for every imaginable contingency, I wasn't sure if there would be any room left for me in the cabin once we brought all of her stuff on board.

There are no "formal nights" on *Trixie*. So why did she ask which suit I had packed?

~ ~ ~ ~ ~ ~

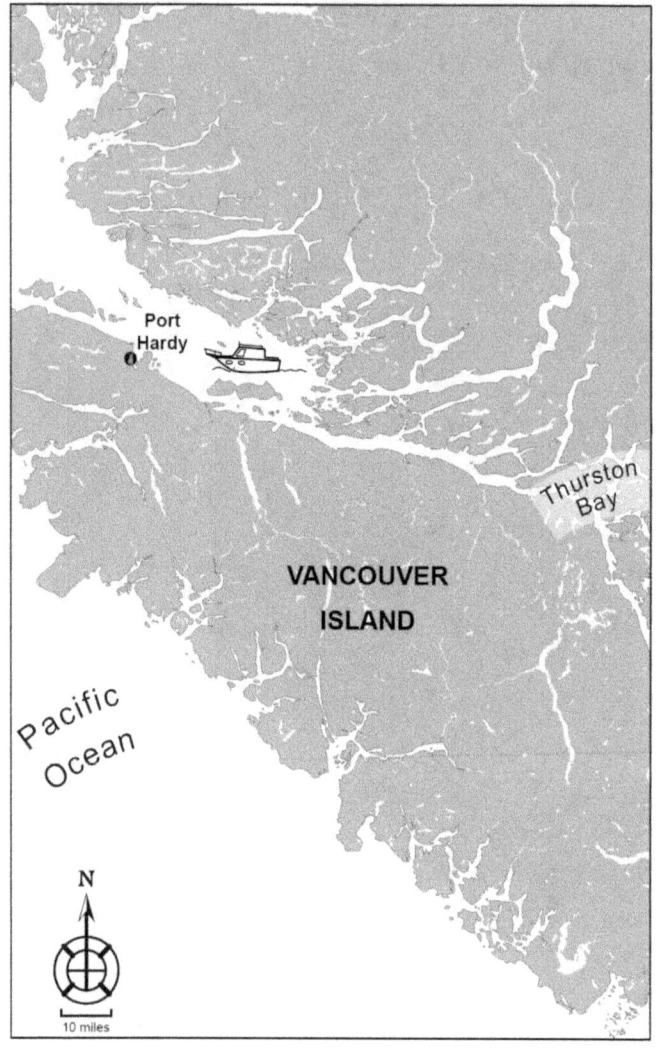

THURSTON BAY to PORT HARDY

Port Hardy

Thurston Bay

VANCOUVER ISLAND

Pacific Ocean

N

10 miles

31: Thurston Bay

I wonder, is it possible to absorb too much beauty?

Leaving Nanaimo the next morning, we continued our way north up the Strait of Georgia, and then later into Discovery Passage. Throughout the day we had the sights of Vancouver Island off our port side and the sights of the British Columbia mainland and its majestic ridge of snow-capped mountains off to starboard.

But you can admire such beauty and wilderness just so long. After a while, it became monotonous. Hour after hour of unsurpassed splendor, not only the natural beauty, but also each town we passed had its own charm. On our port side, we saw numerous villages and towns such as Royston and Oyster River. We rarely came in close to them; mostly we stayed out from the shoreline so as to avoid obstacles such as smaller boats or floating logs.

And, I would swear that some whales were about to commit honorable hari-kari. Those whales were close!

When we came to the large Vancouver, BC, town of Campbell River, we pulled in. We each wanted to get off the boat for a while and walk around on dry land. None of us were used to spending hour upon hour on a boat of this size. It was going to take some getting used to. Being able to stop into a convenient marina and walk around some was a nice change of pace.

I even bought a Campbell River sweatshirt which had the name of the town and the picture of a bear. It had been cold up on deck and I hadn't dressed warmly enough. The sweatshirt would be a great help.

After this, we were off to our destination for the night, Thurston Bay Marine Provincial Park on a mid-size island between Vancouver Island and the mainland. This was just one of many islands in an area that had more islands than I could ever have imagined. I certainly had studied the map but seeing those dots on a map is very different from watching all of those islands pass by.

Waterfalls, elk, floating fish farms, eagles, streams emptying into the bays, seals, whales, schools of fish, small boats pulled up into tree-lined coves, large cargo ships, and rocky outcroppings. Complete beauty.

Reaching Thurston Bay would give us our desired one hundred mile journey for the day, and it would give us our first experience of spending a night while at anchor in a protected cove, instead of at a marina.

I was nervous about this. We had only dropped and raised the anchor twice, and that was just to test it out.

How would we know that the anchor was actually holding us securely and we weren't drifting out into the bay during the night as we slept?

Around six o'clock we reached our destination. Only two other craft, both small sailboats, were there and they were anchored well away from us.

We dropped anchor in a likely spot. Nothing. With the engines off, *Trixie* just drifted about on her own. The anchor obviously had not caught onto anything. So, we moved a bit closer in toward shore and tried again. This time the anchor held.

Seeing a rocky beach about fifty yards away, Charlie and I decided to lower the tender and go explore the island while Scott was preparing dinner, this time with Dawn working as his sous chef. Scott had purchased salmon from the store in Campbell River and we were all looking forward to it.

We probably could have just dipped a line into the water in any random spot on our journey to catch some fish, but none of us had thought to bring fishing equipment onboard. This would likely be rectified when we stopped and refueled at Port Hardy the next day.

I was glad we had practiced working with the tender back in Anacortes. As a result of knowing what to do, we had no problems at all in attaching the tender to the crane, working the crane, and safely lowering it into the water on the starboard side. Once this was done, and with the tender still tethered, we started up the small motor. It worked perfectly. This done, we released the lines and had a leisurely and short ride to the shoreline.

The folks in the closest sailboat were friendly. As Charlie and I walked along the rocky shore in search of a trail to take us inland, two people from the sailboat waved heartily while calling out to us. We couldn't hear what they were saying, so both Charlie and I just waved back.

After a bit, we found a trail as desired. This was another opportunity to get out and move around on dry land and my sea legs needed it. The trail, which was little more than a deer path, led up into a fairly dark copse of pines. The fresh scent was a delight and a nice change from the salt air.

Turns out, the people on the sailboat weren't just being nice when they were waving to us. They were trying to save our butts!

We had gone only thirty or forty yards up that dark, pine-scented trail when we saw movement ahead of us. Stopping to take in the scenery, I pulled out my camera in the hopes of catching a close-up of an elk.

I hadn't expected to take close-up shots of a brown bear family!

Charlie and I froze as we looked ahead of us to see a mother bear and two cubs beside the trail. If I had been at a zoo to see this, I would have enjoyed watching them. Not so much here.

We needed to get out of there! But I had also heard that you should never run when around them. Doing so would just make them think you are prey.

We were prey, and I didn't like that feeling one bit!

Then, momma bear growled. Loudly! We definitely needed to get out of there.

I started to slowly turn so we could retrace our steps and hopefully not alarm the mother bear.

Charlie does squeal like my little sister!

As I was trying to not startle the bear, Charlie had chosen to run for his life, leaving me there darn near within claw slashing distance from the bear as he thrashed toward the rocky shore in panic.

Thanks a lot, Charlie!

Another growl! Holy crap!

Turns out that I can run faster than Charlie can. I passed him just as the two of us broke out of the dark forest, with the bay now just a few yards ahead.

Should I dive into the cold, make that *damn* cold, bay? Should I turn left, and race toward the tender, which we had dragged onto the rocks? I chose the cold water. Charlie chose to turn left to race to the tender fifty yards away.

The folks in the sailboat were cheering us on. Or, maybe they were cheering for the bear. I wasn't sure which.

Five seconds later, Charlie had to follow my example. The bear was rapidly closing on him and there was no way he would reach the tender without having his butt chewed by that angry beast. He turned in a blind panic to run over the slippery and rough rocks as he splashed his way into the water.

Bears can swim. I had forgotten that. It wasn't until I was fully into the water that I remembered it.

Maybe going into the water wasn't such a great idea.

Luckily, the bear didn't seem to care, or maybe she wasn't in the mood for a swim. She stood on the shore and looked out to us as we tried to sink low in the chest-high water and look invisible.

That beautiful creature, seeing that we were no longer a threat, simply turned her back on Charlie and me and went back to the deer trail.

Bears do shit in the woods! I saw her do it as she walked away from us.

~ ~ ~ ~ ~ ~

32: Salmon Anyone?

A young couple from the sailboat rescued us by coming over in kayaks. We couldn't climb on to the kayaks with them, but Charlie and I were each able to hold on as we ventured into deeper water and that helped. We weren't about to drown, but the bear could still come back, if she so chose, and having the kayaks at hand might just save us.

In the meantime, a second couple from the sailboat had worked their way over to our tender in their own bright orange kayaks and I watched as one of them got out of his small craft and stepped into the water to free our tender so it could be floated our way.

A few moments later, Charlie and I were back in our tender, drenched and freezing. That water is cold!

I had also lost another co-captain's cap, just as Charlie had lost his captain's cap. I could see both of them floating away toward the channel. No problem. At last count, I had at least three more co-captain's caps in the hanging locker in my cabin. I thought that Charlie had purchased way too many of them, but at the rate I had been losing my caps, I could now see how those extras might just come in handy.

Dawn and Scott had tuned into what was going on and they were there to greet us when we finally found our way back to *Trixie's Destiny*. Thankfully, they took over the work of managing the tender and getting it back into its cradle on the top deck. I couldn't have done it then, nor could Charlie. We were both shivering and miserable.

Scott invited the other couples from the sailboat to join us for dinner but they both passed up the opportunity. A shame, they had rescued Charlie and me, and they had seemed like nice people.

Chalk up that event to one more thing I was unlikely to tell my wife. I could imagine my next call with her, "Yes, honey, we are having a great time. No, what was that? Of course not, we're just enjoying nature, up close and personal." Yep, that was how the call needed to go.

Warm, dry clothes and a hot shower and I felt human again. Many of our wet things went into the small washing machine located in the hall outside of my cabin to be tended to later.

It was time to eat.

Our first dinner on *Trixie's Destiny*. Up until now, all of our dinners had been in various ports-of-call. Also, I was shaken from the close call with the bear, and this somehow made me even hungrier.

Scott's cooking is superb. Salmon dinner, a logical choice for our location and something I loved.

One irony was that he had purchased it from a store in Campbell River, but only a quarter-mile across the channel from us was one of the largest floating fish farms I had ever seen. It was huge and I would guess that tens of thousands of salmon were in there, just waiting to be put on someone's table.

Regardless of the source, the dinner was incredible. Dawn had worked up salads with pasta for us and had set out wine. It was a total delight. Maybe I should have brought a suit for formal night after all. This service and this wonderful setting there in the pilothouse was top drawer.

After cleaning up the dinner, I went down to my cabin and slept like a log. I wasn't even bothered by Charlie's snoring next door.

Toward morning, the increased movement of the boat woke me. I could easily have slept longer.

Increased movement?

We were in the middle of a protected cove, and water movement was minimal, except for tides which we had accounted for. There shouldn't be this sort of movement, unless another boat had come close and was generating a recurring wake.

We had heard of many boats that were grounded or stuck in the mud as a result of the captain not paying attention to tidal charts. That, at least, we had done.

Concerned, I put on my new sweatshirt with the picture of the bear on it, chuckling at how apropos that was. Then, properly attired, I went up to the main deck to see what had the water churning about so. I also had thoughts of my first coffee for the day.

I turned on the Keurig in the galley, and then stepped out to the side deck to check things out.

We had floated out of the protected cove!

Trixie's Destiny was far from where we had set anchor in the cove the evening before and we had drifted to the middle of the channel. The tidal currents were slowly moving us along toward a neighboring island.

It would seem that while we had paid ample attention to how low a tide might go, we hadn't paid enough attention to how high the tide would get. My best guess was that, while we slept, the tide had risen enough to cause our anchor to slip. As a result, we simply drifted along with the anchor dangling in deep water with nothing to hook onto.

Thankfully, we were not in a shipping lane. Also, thankfully, we were not grounded.

Where we were, was heading smack dab toward the salmon farm. That huge floating facility had a small building attached, and I soon realized that it housed several workers.

I knew this because two of them were running along the center beam which held the gigantic fish cages and were frantically waving us away.

In a few minutes, we would be coming up on that facility and damage to both our boat and the fish farm was a real possibility. The currents were carrying us along at a good clip. If we did bump into the fish farm, it wouldn't be gentle.

I quickly poked my head back into the pilothouse and yelled down to Scott and Charlie that we had an emergency.

Not waiting for them, I went to the lower helm and fired up the engines. Those diesel engines are great. The response was as desired and soon they were ready to push us out of harm's way.

Trixie wouldn't move!

I could only guess that the anchor was holding us back. Somehow, the anchor was allowing us to drift in one direction, across the channel and toward the fish farm, but not allowing us to move in the other direction. Were we caught on something? I'm not sure if I understood how this could work, but I didn't have time to figure it out just then.

In a panic, I pressed the loud horn in the hopes of waking up everyone on board. My earlier yell didn't seem to have done the trick. I needed help!

Soon, Dawn, Scott and Charlie were all up in the pilothouse with me, and they quickly assessed the situation.

Scott took over the controls to the anchor, trying to get that heavy object to cooperate and move.

No luck. It was stuck.

We drifted closer to the fish farm.

Charlie ran to the forepeak and jerked on the windlass, which was keeping the anchor from pulling free.

It worked. Between Scott's and Charlie's efforts, the anchor finally could be reeled in.

I didn't wait for it to come all of the way up. We had to get away from that gigantic floating fish farm!

Quickly, I spun the joystick so that we were pointed away from the hatchery and then gunned it.

Neither the fish farm nor our boat were any longer in danger.

Dawn, on the other hand, was in the water.

She had been putting out the fenders in the hope it might help if we were to collide with the fish farm. My quick start and forward thrust caught her just as she was leaning out to place a fender and she was pitched over.

This all seemed far too familiar. Maybe it was simply her turn.

At least she hadn't been wearing her co-captain's cap.

~ ~ ~ ~ ~ ~

33: Green War Emeralds

We made it to Port Hardy after a long day of cruising the one hundred miles up Johnstone Strait, taking no stops along the way. This had been nearly seven hours on our yacht and it had been non-stop. There were many wonderful sights along the way, but we all wanted to get into port. I even wanted to do a bit of shopping, fishing gear seemed in order. I also wanted to add to my sweatshirt collection...just not one with a bear on it this time.

Port Hardy is a rugged fishing and logging town near the northern tip of Vancouver Island. This would be our last stop along this stretch before we cut across Queen Charlotte Sound where we would come to a vast array of islands forming the western border of British Columbia.

We arrived at the Port Hardy marina, and our reserved slip, mid-afternoon. Once there, we prepared for the next three days' journeys by refueling, replenishing the fresh water, and pumping out the holding tanks...the yucky stuff from the toilets and such.

We also needed to do a bit of grocery shopping. There wouldn't be many stores along this next, long stretch which had no large towns to speak of, just a few small villages. We were going into a desolate area and needed to be prepared for it and needed to stock up.

During the long, uneventful ride up to Port Hardy, Dawn hadn't spoken to me for the first hour or so. She was ticked that I had dumped her into the cold bay. Rather like I had been with Charlie the two times he had dumped me in.

This was getting old and had long ago ceased to be funny. Now it was only Scott that hadn't had the fun of being dunked in unexpectedly. I would have done something about that, except he is way bigger than I am. Dumping him would be funny, although potentially dangerous to my health. Dumping me, Charlie or Dawn was no longer needed.

After doing our shopping, we found a pizza place a short walk from our rented slip and headed that way. On the walk over, Dawn turned on her cellphone and saw that she had a message from Detective Lane in Port Angeles. After listening to the brief message, she immediately called him back.

What she learned during the call was interesting and disturbing to all of us. On the up side, we now knew why Roger Amund and Herbert Langton had been killed.

Emeralds.

Specifically, Colombian Emeralds.

It seems that there is a bit of an ongoing conflict there regarding the mining and distribution of emeralds extracted in the mountains around Bogota.

They call it the "Green War," and both Roger and Herbert were dead because of it.

To be more precise, they were dead because of their own greed. The two men were successful importers of gemstones. Roger owned distribution rights in Washington and Oregon, while Herbert had the western Canadian rights.

The two of them had worked closely together, and both of them loved boating. It was during one of these boating trips when they met in Port Townsend and hatched a plan to further their profits. Apparently being able already to afford a multi-million dollar yacht, *Trixie's Destiny*, wasn't enough for Roger.

Their plan was to cut out the middleman, work directly with the mine owners in Colombia, and greatly increase their margins as a result.

They were also dead. The result of Colombian emerald distributors finding out what our two "friends" were up to.

"Okay," I said slowly to Dawn as I finished a slice of pizza after listening to all of this, "this still leaves a lot of unanswered questions."

"But I think we know what the 'it' is that Viktor Jairo was referring to. Emeralds," Charlie joined in.

Dawn nodded in agreement. "The detective did a good job of interrogating Viktor. It seems that he had been on the periphery of the whole thing and had worked with Roger and Herbert through parts of the process. But, like Roger and Herbert, he too grew greedy and wanted a bigger cut, which was refused to him."

I continued to work on my pizza as Dawn continued to fill in the story.

"So, he went to take the emeralds from the boat for himself, only to find that they were hidden somewhere. Stashing the emeralds onto *Trixie's Destiny* and *Smooth Seas* had been the sole domain of the two, now dead, men. When Viktor went to confront Roger, he found him dead in the head of *Trixie*, and he had a pretty good idea as to who had done it, so he hightailed it out of there."

"And, he came to my boat on family day to find the emeralds?" Charlie asked.

"Exactly," Dawn confirmed.

"So, Viktor, and perhaps bad guys from Colombia, are looking to get their hands on a passel of emeralds, and they think they may be on our boat?" Scott asked with aston-ishment.

"A fortune in emeralds, apparently," Dawn confirmed. "According to Viktor, he thinks we are talking about tens of millions of dollars in value."

"Holy crap!" Scott exclaimed.

"And, they're on *Trixie*?" I asked.

Dawn just nodded.

"How did they get on to my boat in the first place?" Charlie asked, his worry obvious.

"Viktor says that Roger and Herbert were taking turns in heading out to sea to meet up with some other guy from Colombia who had his own boat and they would transfer them there. They aren't sure about this though. There is some conjecture that they might have been meeting a floatplane out in some remote water. We don't know."

She paused for a moment, letting us all absorb what she had said so far. "Bottom-line, someway-somehow, Roger ended up with his hands on a large quantity of emeralds with the goal of making a lot of money, and those emeralds which had been on *Trixie's Destiny* and *Smooth Seas* stayed there before Roger or Herbert were ever able to do anything with them."

"I know the inspector and detective looked through *Trixie* back in Anacortes," Scott said, "but maybe not well enough, plus they didn't know what they were looking for. It now sounds like we need to conduct an emerald search."

"Also, it sounds like we have some pissed-off Colombians who want their emeralds and they don't mind killing people to get them," Dawn summarized.

We all mulled this over for a bit and then Dawn laid a big one on us. "We're going to have another 'co-captain' for the rest of our trip north."

"What!" Charlie exclaimed.

"Detective Lane got in touch with Inspector Gibson from Victoria, and the inspector wants to come along. It seems he has hopes of being onboard when the bad guys try to come and get us. He would also like to find the emeralds and take them in custody and do so with a lot of press so that the bad guys will know that they are no longer on *Trixie*."

"Any chance that he just wants them for himself?" I asked. This scenario sounded fishy.

"Doubtful. But, if he does want the emeralds, he can have them."

"As long as he doesn't try to whack us in the process," Charlie said, his fear obvious.

"We can guard against that... I hope. Anyway, it will be well known that Inspector Gibson is on the boat with us. Detective Lane is making sure of that. The inspector would be foolish to try and steal them for himself. There is no way he could keep it secret."

"Good point, and I'm glad to know that Detective Lane will help if needed."

"Darn right. I trust the Detective, plus the inspector seems like a good guy. I have a pretty good ability to read people, after all," Dawn added, referring to her years as a successful detective.

"Okay," I joined in, my pizza largely done, "he asked to join our little crew and you said yes."

"We're in Canadian waters, his territory, so I couldn't very well say no," she turned to Charlie, "Sorry, I probably should have checked with you first, it's your boat, after all."

"That's okay. I would have agreed with it, just like you did," he said forlornly as he picked at a piece of pepperoni lying askew on his pizza.

"We don't have any room!" I added, knowing full well that I didn't want to share my small cabin with a stranger. "This is just for the northbound part of the trip, not for the return leg when we have the four others with us, right?"

"Not sure," Dawn responded. "Oh, he can sleep on the sleeper-sofa in the main deck salon. According to him, this would be a luxury compared to most of the boats he has crewed on."

"I don't like this," Scott complained.

"We don't have a choice," Dawn said. "He will be here first thing in the morning. He's coming up on a floatplane from Victoria and will meet us out by Duval Island, just a short ride from here. It seems that he doesn't want anyone on land to see him come aboard."

This too, I knew, wasn't likely to be relayed to my wife. "Yes dear, we are having a lovely time, dear. And, no dear, we aren't having any problems at all." Yes, that was going to be my next call with her.

Right after that, I might just want to review my will.

~ ~ ~ ~ ~ ~

34: Fishing Weapons

As planned, the next morning we came to the far side of Duval Island where we were out of sight from anyone on Vancouver Island and Port Hardy. We had to wait less than fifteen minutes before we saw a sturdy de Havilland floatplane make its approach.

Watching that rugged aircraft fascinated me. The flight training I had taken years before involved nothing like this. All of my practice flights had been from local airports and in a small Cessna. We would fly over houses and cornfields in Ohio, and then make our way back to a paved strip.

Not these guys. There was no airstrip. There were no markings to guide them. Just water. Water that could be quite bumpy. There also weren't any of the navigation aids available when coming into a "normal" airport, nor any guidance regarding obstacles, wind patterns, or flight traffic patterns.

To land the floatplane, they had to circle the area, look for any boats that might be problematic, check out the wave condition, take a guess at wind direction, hope there weren't any logs or whales about to pop up in their path, and then bring the plane down.

That would have scared the crap out of me.

Luckily, the water was fairly smooth. If it hadn't been, the pilot would have to choose either making an unsafe landing near us, or landing closer into Port Hardy...which the inspector did not want.

The pilot made it all look easy.

Now, we had to get the inspector from the plane and into our boat, and do so out in the water, away from prying eyes.

In preparation, we had our tender down in the water, ready to come over to the plane once the engine was shut off and the propellers were not a threat to us. I was enjoying working with the tender and motoring that small craft around. I stood at the controls, and with Dawn to help, we watched the plane expertly come to a stop less than forty yards from us. We waited as the pilot shut off the one engine.

Within moments I'd brought the tender alongside one of the plane's pontoons and Inspector Gibson handed out two bags, which Dawn took, and then he stepped into our bobbing tender as if it was something he did every day.

Perhaps he did.

Hellos were said and soon we had him on board and the tender back up into its cradle on the top deck. The pilot wasted no time. He had turned the engine back on and was up out of the water as soon as we were safely away from the de Havilland.

As the inspector stepped from the tender and up into *Trixie's Destiny*, Scott and Charlie were there to present him with a new Co-Captain cap. I cringed, wondering what he would say. He loved it and proudly placed it on his head. That one small act immediately gave us a favorable impression of him. So, *Trixie* was now crewed by a seasick-prone captain and four co-captains.

Breakfast. He had brought a collection of pastries from the Empress Hotel, plus he had his own supply of tea bags. He was definitely a "Brit" at heart. I just didn't want to tell him that we didn't have a teakettle on board. We didn't even have any tea for the Keurig.

Score one big demerit in cross-border relationships for us.

While breakfast was being prepared, Charlie had navigated us through a set of small islands. Luckily, the water was smooth for this first leg. We had half a chance of Charlie being able to keep his breakfast down.

Soon, we were through the islands and headed out across the Queen Charlotte Sound and open sea toward Calvert Island. Once at Calvert Island, we would be out of the sound and able to stay within the shelter of a long chain of islands.

We were following the course taken by the BC Ferries. Every day they plied these waters, stopping at a few towns along the way such as Port Hardy. We had seen one head out before us that morning; its destination was Prince Rupert, the same port we were planning to visit in three days.

We were also skirting the edge of our first "blue water"…the open ocean. We would be in that deep water, away from any shoreline, for nearly sixty miles. The closest we had come to this type of boating before was our trip to Port Townsend, a much more protected area. The wind out in the Queen Charlotte sound didn't help either. It forced us to stay inside and navigate from the pilothouse and not from the fly bridge, which had all of that wonderful fresh air.

That wind also picked up the waves. We weren't in danger, but it wasn't a smooth ride either. We had the stabilizers on, which helped a little, but the boat was still rocking and rolling about. After a short while of this, Charlie silently handed the controls over to me, causing me to wonder if he was having trouble with the boat's motions in that choppy water.

Charlie was definitely having problems.

As this was going on, Scott and Dawn were sitting at the table near the helm with Inspector Gibson, I never did hear his first name…unless his parents actually gave him the first name of "Inspector." They watched as Charlie darted out the portside door, only to spew forth that great breakfast that Scott had prepared, along with the scones and pastries the inspector had given to us.

After the incident with the McBeignets weeks ago, I would have hoped Charlie would have learned his lesson. It seems he hadn't. Simple equation for Charlie: pastries + rolling seas = puke. He hadn't yet done the math.

Charlie was embarrassed. He was the owner of this expensive yacht and he was our "captain." Now, he was presenting the inspector with his worst side. Literally. For a long while, his butt protruded toward us as he leaned over the side rail and continued on his own personal rapid-weight-loss program.

The port side of the boat was going to need cleaning. Again.

Tiring of watching this, Scott, Dawn and the Inspector started conducting a search for the emeralds. This had been done before, but it was time to do it again. Hopefully, now that they knew what they were looking for, they might find something.

I called out to remind Charlie about chewing on some ginger and he darted from the outside side rail into the galley to retrieve a piece.

Charlie suddenly had a bothersome thought. With extremely foul breath, he came up close to me and whispered, "Guns! He will find our weapons!"

"Oh shit," was all I could mutter. Charlie was right. We had stashed numerous weapons of various types throughout *Trixie*. We had also flat-out lied when going through Canadian customs, declaring that we didn't have any firearms with us.

Even though Scott had been the one who first wanted to hide all of those weapons on board, knowing that Canada had strict firearms regulations, actually lying to customs went against everything he believed in. He really had not thought this through.

We had hidden the weapons to protect our asses from bad guys...not to lie to other officials. In the end, he relented. He had wanted the weapons on board, as did Dawn, so they remained, even with the emotional conflict this caused.

With the search for emeralds on, the inspector was bound to find some of our weapons, and much of what we had was illegal in Canada. If we were still in Canadian waters. I wasn't sure.

Searching through the main salon for the stash of emeralds, with Dawn and Scott at his side, the inspector inevitably found one of the automatic weapons. This one had been hidden in the couch, the very couch he would be sleeping on that night.

"Crap," I heard Scott exclaim. He was trying to make it look like he had forgotten they were there. It wasn't working. Scott was a horrible liar. We had played poker a few times and he had more "tells" than anyone I had ever known.

I turned from the helm and looked into the salon. I had a decent view from where I sat and could see the three of them talking earnestly down there.

Scott called up to me, "This is special fishing equipment, right Frank?"

Of course it wasn't fishing equipment…unless we were trying to take out a squad of oversized killer sharks, but I caught the drift of the open lie.

I could see the three of them expectantly looking at me, waiting for me to participate.

"Yes, of course. We are hoping to catch some big ones," I added, crossing my fingers for luck. I could imagine another call with my wife, "Yes dear, everything is fine dear. By the way, would you mind coming over to the prison to bail me out?"

Luckily, the inspector didn't seem bent out of shape over the guns. He had, after all, openly gone along with the "guns = fishing equipment" story. To keep a bit of control to this, and perhaps cover his own butt, he warned us indirectly. "If those big ones, you know, 'Colombian Emerald Snappers,' for example, are no longer a threat, you will get rid of this fishing equipment. Won't you?"

"Trust me," I called out while still sitting at the helm with Charlie's puke-tainted breath still fogging up the area, "that fishing equipment will be gone at the first safe opportunity." This had been a unilateral announcement on my part, but we didn't have much choice just then.

I could see the inspector mulling this over further. He probably could have arrested us or made us pitch the weapons overboard. But, he too, knew that there was real danger lurking out there and, being on board with us as he was, he was now also in danger.

"One way or the other, that 'fishing equipment' will be gone from this boat before you get back to Vancouver Island."

"Absolutely," Dawn said.

We dodged that bullet…so to speak.

The search for emeralds continued. The three of them were thorough. Every compartment was searched. Food containers were inspected. Mattresses and cushions checked for hiding spots. Oil cans down in the engine room were checked. Everything, even spaces where no human was ever likely to go. With two detectives among them, they knew all of the tricks and were able to find little hidey-holes which I never would have known existed.

No emeralds were found, and they had checked as thoroughly as any three trained law enforcement professionals could do.

Maybe the damned things had already been found by the Colombians and there actually was no threat. I liked that thought and when I said so to Charlie, his face brightened considerably.

"What about the *Smooth Seas*?" I heard Scott ask the inspector. "Were emeralds found on that boat?"

"No, unfortunately," he said as he sipped a cup of coffee, grimacing at its taste. "Think about it, though. Herbert Langton was killed months after Roger Amund. He had plenty of opportunity to move the emeralds off of *Smooth Seas* in that time."

"Sounds logical," Dawn added.

"Yes and no. Let me counter my own analysis about Langton having plenty of time to move the jewels off of his boat. The interesting thing here is that our undercover people didn't find any hint of a large quantity of new emeralds showing up in Vancouver or Victoria. There has been no word on the street from folks who should know. So, even though Langton could have moved the emeralds, I think there was a chance that Amund's death spooked him and Langton never took his emeralds off of *Smooth Seas*. But we will probably never know."

"If you are right, and if the Colombians did find Langton's share of the jewels on *Smooth Seas*, they would know that Amund had the rest, and they would be after them," Dawn summarized.

"Unfortunately, yes. And, unfortunately, I think that is exactly what may be happening."

Finally, it was time for lunch and time to turn the conversation away from this worrying line of thought. Calvert Island was in sight and we would soon be in the channel to the east of the island, with much calmer water.

The search had been done, and we were looking forward to a full meal.

Everyone, except Charlie. I don't think he ever wanted to see food again.

~ ~ ~ ~ ~ ~

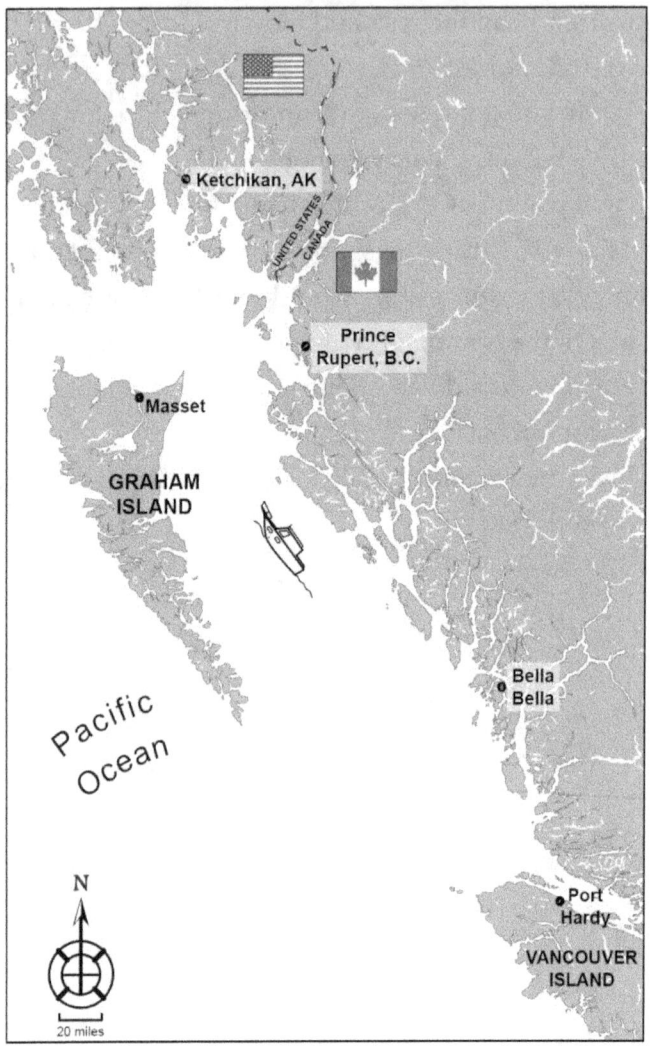

PORT HARDY to KETCHIKAN

Ketchikan, AK

UNITED STATES
CANADA

Prince
Rupert, B.C.

Masset

GRAHAM
ISLAND

Pacific

Ocean

N

20 miles

Bella
Bella

Port
Hardy

VANCOUVER
ISLAND

35: Prince Rupert

Three days later, we arrived in Prince Rupert, British Columbia on a rainy day. Nothing unusual here.

It had been raining for much of the last two days. Visibility was hit and miss, causing us to depend heavily on our navigation screens, along with having a second person keep an eye out for rocky outcroppings, boats or other obstacles while doing this through a gray mist.

The rain and the grayness were unfortunate. We had just passed through some of the most beautiful country on the planet and we couldn't see much of it.

Beautiful, except for the sameness: mountains, animals along the shore, waterfalls, forests, jagged rocky outcroppings, streams, seals, and so on it went. Three days of repetitive, awe-inspiring beauty.

I had stopped taking photos with my digital camera early in the trip. No snapshot could do justice to the place, and no set of snapshots could capture the sense of the remoteness and unending splendor.

Only two things marred this nearly three-day jaunt through the various channels: rain and boredom.

The rain and drizzle kept us inside much of the time. The boredom was a natural extension of sitting on that boat, hour after hour, watching the grey, mist-shrouded, scenery roll past.

The biggest change in scenery was when we would encounter a ferry, freighter, or other yacht. There are many, especially during the summer months. Each time this happened, we would watch the passengers on the ferry wave to us, while we waved back in turn.

Twice, we were flagged down by people on other yachts who simply wanted to chat and to break the monotony. Yachters are friendly and love to share their knowledge of the various coves and places to drop anchor. Each time this happened, Inspector Gibson was at high alert. Being hailed to stop by another boat, while ostensibly a friendly gesture, was also a great way for someone to accost us.

None of that happened. We were in a totally remote set of waterways and it would have been easy for any local bad guy, or the Colombians, to attack us. They didn't.

We had two overnight stays along the way; one in the marina at the small village of Bella Bella, and the second in a small cove near Hartley Bay. After our first night anchoring in a cove and finding that we had broken free from our mooring at night, we were skittish about spending another night secured only by an anchor.

We didn't want for every night to be spent at a marina. They could be noisy, and we had found an inviting, secluded spot. We just had to properly secure *Trixie's Destiny*. Taking great care, we dropped the anchor into an area where we were not likely to run into trouble. We also set up an inspection schedule. Every hour, one of us was to get up and check to ensure that we were still secure.

It all went fine. I had been nervous all night, but my fears were unwarranted.

The highlight was when I caught a fish! Less than an hour after docking in that small cove, I pulled out some of the fancy new fishing gear I had purchased back in Port Hardy, went to the back cockpit, beer in hand, and dropped a line. I had no clue what I was fishing for or what lure or bait to use. It was the experience of fishing out here that mattered.

A King Salmon. That sucker fought hard! Soon, Scott came up to help and, together, we tugged and tussled with that thrashing beauty. Then, pulling it up to take a closer look, along with several pictures, we cut it free. It was a shame, but we simply had no way to clean and cut it up. We also didn't have room in our already crammed freezer.

Plus, we already had a unique dinner for that night. Elk Burgers. Scott had purchased the meat in a shop in the village of Bella Bella the night before. More and more, we were learning what an expert chef Scott was, and we all eagerly helped him, knowing the resulting meal would be delicious.

Sometimes, that extra help can be a bit too much though. In this case, by me. We caught a break in the weather when it came time to prepare dinner, so Scott was able to cook the burgers over the built-in gas grill on the fly bridge instead of the electric stovetop in the galley. Scott had a nice flame going on the grill just as I bumped into him, which then caused a wad of paper towels to hit the flames.

We had a fire. Not much of one, but it sent us all into high gear.

Charlie, our resident fireman, quickly grabbed a fire extinguisher from the galley, ran up the stairway to the fly bridge and aimed it at the small fire, a fire that had almost gone out by itself. This didn't stop Charlie; he wanted to douse everything in sight.

The extinguisher didn't work!

It was a dud. Charlie looked at it and soon determined that the extinguisher was way out of date and needed a recharge. That, and the whole mechanism seemed flawed.

The good news was that there was no need for the extinguisher. The paper towels had flamed out by themselves and soon Scott was back to working on dinner.

After that event, things went back to normal and we prepared for the next leg north.

Finally, we arrived in Prince Rupert. Inspector Gibson was scheduled to get off here. No surprise, this was almost as far north as you could go along the coast and still be in Canada. He didn't want to be on board our yacht when it reentered the U.S.

The inspector was scheduled to spend a few days with his counterpart in that lonely part of the world for some cross training. Three days later, we were to come and pick him up again for the return voyage.

We had an arrangement. After leaving Prince Rupert, we were to head up to Ketchikan, and the U.S., which was slightly under a day's travel. Francine, Sally, Janet and Dawn's special friend, Tony, were going to meet us there.

I wanted to play tourist for a day in Ketchikan. It had been an enjoyable stop when our cruise ship visited a while back, and I knew there was still much to see. Then, we would come back to Prince Rupert to pick up the inspector.

With him on board, along with our wives and "special friends," the boat would be crowded. There was room, though, but not a lot. The inspector had proven to be just fine in using the pullout sofa bed. Where we ran into problems was with bathrooms. He didn't have one, while each of the cabins and the crew area did. In the end, he chose to use Charlie's, as it was the largest. That had been fine before, but heading south, with Charlie now sharing his cabin with Janet, I wasn't so sure how that would work out.

Worrying about sleeping and bathroom arrangements was a small thing. The big worry was our weapons. We could only hope that no one in U.S. Customs in Ketchikan or Canadian Customs, when we returned to Canada, found our weapons. That would not be a fun situation.

For our remaining hours in Prince Rupert, we were able to get a ride up to a Safeway and stock-up again. This done, we were anxious to get up to Ketchikan.

Alaska. After a week of cruising on *Trixie's Destiny*, we would finally be in Alaska. I couldn't wait.

This was definitely going on my *Facebook* page. Now, I only needed to find out how to create one.

~ ~ ~ ~ ~ ~

36: Ketchikan

We had a greeting committee when we arrived at the marina in Ketchikan. Standing and waving at us on the dock were the four others. I could see my wife, Francine, gaily waving at me as she stood alongside the others. It was rather fun. All that was missing were the balloons or the shore excursion guys waiting to take our pictures alongside a big sign with the name of the port on it.

In addition to my wife on the dock, I could also see two large suitcases. They were hers, I recognized them. I had a matching bag of my own in the same set.

I groaned when I saw those cases.

They had been told which rental slip was ours and had eagerly been waiting for us. Their charter flight had arrived just a few hours before and they wasted no time finding their way across the channel from the airport and over to the dock. They wanted to join us.

Trixie's Destiny was ready for guests. We had been cleaning and tidying the boat for all of the nearly eighty-mile trip up from Prince Rupert. We even now had a teakettle, courtesy of Inspector Gibson, who had picked it up for us before we headed out that morning.

Soon, with hugs and excited greetings, we had all four of our guests on board. All of them, except Janet, were familiar with *Trixie* so only Janet needed to be given a tour. Janet, a delightful, mature woman, who seemed to be a perfect match for Charlie, was proudly shown around by our good captain.

We also presented each of them with caps proudly stating that each of our guests were "co-co-captains." Really. But this time Charlie was being purposefully playful.

With the caps placed on our guest's heads, we then stowed their luggage in the cabins.

I was pleasantly surprised. At least half of what my wife had packed could be stashed in my small cabin.

She was far less happy with the situation than I was, but we worked it out and the half-full suitcases were finally packed into spare compartments in Charlie's very large owner's cabin. It would be a bit awkward, but with all of the stuff she had packed, it was all we could do.

Accepting as she was of the cabin and the lack of storage, her reaction to the lack of available space in my bathroom/head was almost funny.

Not funny to her, though. It didn't take long for Francine to check out the larger cabin and head that Scott was using. Everything she had brought on board would have fit in there. That glare told me that she wasn't impressed with my choice of cabins.

She especially wouldn't be impressed with my choice of cabins once she got to listen to Charlie snoring at night through the thin cabin walls. I decided to hold back on that delightful bit of news.

Finally, we were unpacked, and we all gathered in the main salon for a welcome aboard drink. Only Tony was wearing his new "co-co-captain" cap. It seems that the other three were not quite so willing to wear them.

It was time to hit the town. Ketchikan is long and narrow as it hugs along the rocky coast. We were docked about mid-point, and our goal was to hit the prime tourist area which was near one end. Given that this was the middle of summer, and there were three large cruise ships in town, I knew that things were going to be crowded.

It was, but it was almost fun. After days of cruising on *Trixie's Destiny* through the wilderness, and seeing very few other humans along the way, being around this mass of camera-toting vacationers was a welcome change of pace.

We braved the crowds and I found my way to a booth at the dock that sold shore excursions. Last time I was here, we had taken a floatplane flight out for a crab feast at a remote lodge. Now, I wanted to take a jeep adventure up backcountry roads. It sounded fun.

Scott chose to go with me on that excursion the next morning, while the others simply wanted to remain in town and explore the many shops.

Our plan was to spend the entire next day playing tourist, spend a second night docked at the Ketchikan marina, and the following morning we would head back to Prince Rupert where we would pick up the inspector.

Inspector Gibson. That was going to be an interesting discussion. None of our four guests knew about him or why he would be with us. I imagined yet another conversation with Francine," Yes, honey. We will have a Provincial Inspector on board to help guard against attack from the Colombians. What's that? I hadn't told you that we might have an angry pack of Colombians on our ass? Gee, I'm not sure how that could have slipped my mind."

This was definitely going to be fun.

Somehow, we managed to skirt the topic almost completely during dinner. All that was said was we were going to stop at Prince Rupert as our first port of call, where we would check in with customs and a friend might be stopping in to see us.

That last statement from Scott should have raised all sorts of questions from any of our four guests, but it didn't.

During dinner, we got to know Janet. She was new to everyone in the group except Charlie. Lovely lady, and I think Charlie did well in finding her.

"Speaking of you two getting together," Dawn brought up during dinner, "how did that happen exactly? Charlie said something about a grocery store?"

Janet went on to gaily describe how she had seen Charlie at the Safeway in Anacortes several times and thought he was cute.

"Cute?" I laughed, causing my wife to kick me.

"He is…just look at those big, puppy-dog eyes?" Janet playfully responded.

Francine kicked me again before I could respond to the "puppy-dog eyes" comment. My shin was starting to hurt.

Finally, we got the full story out of her and learned how she had built up the courage to "accidentally" bump into him with her shopping cart. That first time had no effect and he didn't pay her any attention, so a few minutes later she did it again. This second time, Charlie finally twigged.

That last part made sense. I could see Charlie being a bit slow to tune into the attentions of an attractive mature woman like Janet. He had only ever dated his wife, and she was now deceased. Put another way, Charlie was totally clueless when it came to women.

Put yet another way, every guy is totally clueless when it comes to women. Charlie just happened to have a graduate degree on the subject.

During dinner, Janet was very curious about the up-coming voyage, asking numerous questions about every facet of life aboard *Trixie's Destiny*. She was especially interested in the planned route and both Charlie and I gladly obliged by pulling out the map app on our smart phones to show her how we had worked our way north to Ketchikan and what we were considering for our return with them back to Anacortes.

It was fun. We enjoyed sharing our experiences and were all looking forward to a fun week together as we headed back home.

The next day was tourist day. Scott and I took that enjoyable Jeep tour of the backcountry, along with a bunch of folks fresh off of a cruise ship. I was even able to add another sweatshirt to my collection. This one with a jeep, a forest and a moose on it. No bears. That last one with the bear had been a bad omen.

Charlie, Dawn and Tony spent the morning at the marina refueling *Trixie*, along with refreshing her water supplies and emptying out the sump and other nastiness. Janet, Francine and Sally spent the day enjoying the quaint tourist area in Ketchikan, following this up with grocery shopping.

Scott was ticked off when he found that they had done grocery shopping for our boat without checking with him first. He was the cook, not them.

I wondered just how long that arrangement would hold. It was starting to seem like we might now have several cooks, each with "Type-A" personalities.

We had all chosen to eat at local restaurants for breakfast and dinner. Later, we could figure out how to cook for, and feed, all eight of us. There was one eating table, and it only held four. I stopped worrying about it. We now had four co-co-captains to figure it all out.

We were ready for a week of cruising south, on what was starting to feel like a very crowded boat.

Now, if I could just figure out which of my wife's clothes were in my cabin, and which ones were still in suitcases stuffed into Charlie's cabin.

~ ~ ~ ~ ~ ~

37: Oh, That's Where They Are

Departing out of Ketchikan after two nights there was a bit of a circus. Prior to this, our foursome, plus Inspector Gibson, pretty well knew who-does-what onboard and we had a good division of duties. Now, we had four more people and they all wanted to help.

We were stumbling all over each other.

Scott, our chef of choice, soon had my wife and Sally in the small galley to "help." Given that Sally was his wife, he couldn't say no. The three of them had distinctly different styles and protocols for how absolutely everything should be done. I think the tension there in that kitchen generated a whole new force field which could have been sensed for miles.

Dawn, Tony and I managed the fenders and lines, pulling them in while Charlie took us out from Ketchikan. Tony tried to help with the lines, but we had to redo everything he did. I also don't think we will ever find the forward starboard fender again. Who knows where he stashed it.

Charlie had Janet right by his side to watch his every move as they sat up in the covered fly bridge, navigating *Trixie's Destiny* out of Ketchikan and then south. Luckily, all of the cruise ships that were destined to make port that morning had already found their way up the channel, so we didn't have to work around them.

Charlie was darned good at navigation. This had evolved into his responsibility and he enjoyed it. Janet was now questioning his every move, making suggestions for the best course to take. Was there trouble in paradise already?

She was already requesting that we take a different course south. We were planning on staying inside the channels and head to Prince Rupert. Janet wanted, and soon cajoled Charlie into choosing, a different path. This new course would have us follow the same route taken by the cruise ships for the first part. This would be okay, except we would be into rougher waters and heading to an entirely new location.

Our new destination for our first day was to be the fishing village of Masset, at the northern tip of Graham Island, about three or four hours away and a good distance from Prince Rupert. Janet said that her sister was a schoolteacher there, and that she had wanted to see where her sister lived ever since she had moved. The two of them had even planned a cookout at her home.

That seemed okay, although it changed our plans. But, being able to visit with a person who lived in one of these remote villages, and who could show us around, was appealing.

The big problem here was that we wouldn't be picking up Inspector Gibson as promised. That pick-up would have to wait a day. It could also cause our return to be a day later than planned. No problem for the retired folks in the group, but Tony and Sally both still worked. I thought that Janet also worked in real estate, but this possible delay didn't bother her.

While we had cruised southward through the channel and away from Ketchikan, a feast was being prepared down in the galley by Scott, Sally and Francine. They ended up cooking enough for way more people than we had on board.

Scott was totally stressing over this as he could see how our supply of food would run out before we made it home. He kept trying to tell Sally and Francine this, but he wasn't being heard. They seemed to think that we could just pop into grocery stores at any point along the way.

My guess was we would be stocking up at the grocery in Prince Rupert, if we now ever saw that port, given the change of plans caused by Janet. At the rate we were going through food, after just one meal, we wouldn't last more than three days. Maybe we could make it all of the way back to Port Hardy without replenishing our stores, but Scott wasn't so sure.

Finally, the huge meal was ready. We ate in different groups. Four people at the table in the pilothouse and four of us topside. Charlie, Janet, Francine and I had taken our meals to the fly bridge, which allowed Charlie to eat as he navigated the yacht. By the time breakfast was served, we had passed through the channel to the north and west of Annette Island, a large Indian reservation. Soon, we would be heading out to much more open water. Blue water.

Janet, who had dished up the meals for Charlie and herself, had selected a set of jelly-filled pastries for each of them. A token of affection from her, but I wanted to warn her that it was a bad idea. Especially given the rougher waters we were entering.

I watched Charlie chow down on that large pastry and cringed. He still hadn't done the "pastries + rough water = puke" math. As he finished a mouthful, I heard Charlie disclose information on Inspector Gibson to Janet and how we needed to call him to let him know we wouldn't be coming in until the next day.

This naturally raised several questions from Francine and Janet. Who was Inspector Gibson and why would he be joining us?

Well, Charlie had just opened that can of worms. Someone had to sooner or later so having the dread news come from our captain seemed reasonable. I sat back and let him fill in the blanks for our guests. First, he needed to let the inspector know about our change in plans.

With Janet sitting at the helm beside Charlie, the three of us listened as Charlie got on the marine phone and contacted Inspector Gibson at the number we had been given. I couldn't hear the conversation but soon learned the results.

"He says it's okay. He can come over to Masset on one of their helicopters."

Not a bad job when you can call up the services of a floatplane or helicopter at a moment's notice. I can't say that working in marketing ever gave me that privilege.

With the call complete, and at Janet's urging, Charlie outlined the basics of who Inspector Gibson was and his rationale for coming aboard *Trixie's Destiny*. Both my wife and Janet went silent.

That silence had daggers laced into it.

Shame on us for not telling them all about this before we ever let them get onto our yacht. That was a dumb move on our part and irresponsible.

Put another way...I would never hear the end of it.

Rightfully so.

Charlie had just finished his big breakfast as the two women mulled this over. He totally wasn't tuning into their reactions to this news. I was. I could feel the tension.

My wife was pissed. How could we do such a thing without telling her?

Janet had a different reaction. I wasn't sure what it was.

I tried to soften the news by describing how we thought the emeralds had already been found by the Colombians and how we didn't have any problems on the way up. In my opinion, there was no likely danger to us.

My wife was still pissed.

Charlie tried to add more comfort to the discussion by reminding them of how we would have a police inspector on board and that it would be a good thing.

Janet, listened to this and seemed to be deep in thought over it as we began to hit some rougher waters. Charlie turned on the stabilizer in an attempt to soften the rolling effect. Stabilizers do a great job, but primarily at low speeds or at a dead stop. We were hoofing along at a pretty good clip, probably around fifteen nautical miles per hour, reducing how effective the stabilizers were.

There was complete silence, uncomfortable silence, for a while up there on that fly bridge. After a while, Janet said she needed to go down to her cabin to get something.

That "something," it turned out, was a gun. I have no idea where she got it. It wasn't one that we had stashed away.

When Janet returned to the fly bridge, she stood at the top of the stairs from the pilothouse below and pointed a pistol at Charlie, and then at Francine and me.

"What the hell!" I exclaimed. Then it hit me. Janet was one of the bad guys. She didn't look Colombian, though. Not that I had a clue as to how a Colombian was supposed to look.

My reaction surprised the other three. I laughed.

"What's so damn funny?" Janet snarled. Suddenly, she was no longer an attractive, mature woman. She was now a threat; all of her feminine charms were long gone.

"You didn't accidentally meet Charlie in the market, did you?" I chuckled. I couldn't help myself, but the absurdity of the situation seemed to warrant it.

"No. Of course not! I made it happen," she responded derisively as she frowned at Charlie. "Trust me; I could do a lot better."

"That's harsh," I said, and then shut up as she pointed the gun at me.

Charlie looked queasy and frightened. As a fireman, he'd handled many stressful situations. Having a gun pointed at him was probably not among them.

My wife simply clutched my hand. Hard. One of the things I admired about her was the way she didn't overre- act. She absorbed, considered the facts, and then acted as the situation warranted. She was now doing just that. I knew her mind was churning rapidly.

"You don't have a sister at Masset or Graham Island, do you?" Francine accused the other woman.

"Nope."

"What's there then? Why are we going there?" My wife asked Janet who was casually waving the gun from Charlie to us and back again.

"It is more a question of what, or who, wasn't supposed to be there that matters. Your friend, Inspector Gibson, for one. I can't have him, or anyone from the Canadian police, around. It would spoil things."

"But he will be there. He's flying in," I said then kicked myself for reminding her of that.

"Not after Charlie calls him and tells him that we decided to come to Prince Rupert after all," Janet stated as she glared at Charlie, expecting him to immediately make a call back to cancel the inspector's trip.

"Do you know him?" I asked, and then I started to wonder where the others were. Janet had closed the hatch between the fly bridge and the pilot house, and this had to make them wonder what was going on.

"I know him by reputation. And, I know that he is on the hunt for my emeralds."

"Your emeralds?"

"My family's emeralds. They belong to us. That guy, Roger Amund, tried to cheat us out of our rights to sell them."

I thought about this. I couldn't begin to contest who had the rights to the emeralds and I didn't care. I just knew that I wanted that gun to be gone, and I wanted Janet the hell off of our boat.

"Those emeralds you are looking for aren't on *Trixie*. We've looked everywhere. Even Inspector Gibson looked and found nothing," I tried to explain to her.

Charlie was saying nothing. If anything, he was looking ill. Given his history, I wouldn't doubt it.

Janet laughed. "The emeralds aren't on this boat? You're a dumb ass." Venom tainted her every word. "They're all over this boat. Just like they were on Langton's boat, the *Smooth Seas*."

"That can't be!" I exclaimed. "If they were on this boat, we would have found them."

"Did you look in the fire extinguishers? That's where they were on *Smooth Seas*. It took a while for the owner of that sailboat to tell us where they were. But, he did, and then, well, he died." She gave a wicked grin as she moved closer to Charlie and leaned into him to ensure that he made the call to Inspector Gibson in time for him to cancel his flight.

Holy crap. We *were* dumb asses. *Trixie's Destiny* was filled with fire extinguishers, far more than necessary. Plus, we knew that at least one of them didn't work — probably because it was stuffed with jewels.

"The extinguishers have the emeralds in them, don't they?" I stated the obvious, half-proud of figuring this out and also ashamed at being so slow.

Her response was unexpected. "What the hell!"

Charlie had thrown up all over her.

True projectile vomit.

~ ~ ~ ~ ~ ~

38: Puke and Bullets

Janet's face and chest were covered with the stuff. Yuck!

While I was cringing at the sight, the hatchway from the pilothouse stairs burst open and Scott ran up, with gun in hand. As he did this, Dawn leapt up from the rear stairway, which led from the cockpit.

They had been lying in wait, hoping for an opportunity, while not wanting to accidentally cause any of us to get shot. Janet was, after all, pointing a loaded weapon at us. At least, I assumed it was loaded.

At the same time, my incredible wife dove for Janet and tackled her! I had been sitting there doing nothing while my wife had analyzed the situation, processed the facts, and did what was needed.

I definitely have to remember to not piss her off the next time I am pondering something dumb.

With Janet down, Scott roughly placed one foot on the hand that held the pistol, while Dawn quickly removed the gun. The threat had been neutralized.

Those three, were incredible, and Francine hadn't even been part of all of those "bad guy drills" we had conducted back in Anacortes.

We now had a situation on our hands and needed to figure out what to do next. I figured we would leave that to our resident experts, Dawn and Scott.

Sally was down below, crying in fright. Tony was standing about, much as I was doing, not knowing what to do, Charlie was ill, and was busily soiling much of the upper helm area while also trying to put *Trixie* into autopilot. And, we had a criminal on our hands. An international, Colombian emerald cartel criminal.

My first act was to hug my wife and praise her again and again.

Her first reaction was to slap me. That pissed-off thing that had been building up since she'd learned how Roger had been killed, and the possibility that some sort of angry Colombian cartel was coming after us, finally came out.

Her second act was to apologize. She had never hit me before and her harsh, physical reaction was unsettling, to say the least.

If I had been in her place, I wouldn't have stopped at one slap. I had deserved it for keeping mum about the possible danger.

Make that, real danger.

Our third act was to hug each other and then turn to look down at the angry woman who lay prone on the teak deck before us.

Scott had scurried down to his cabin while Dawn was watching over Janet. As this was going on, Sally and Tony had come up to the fly bridge to find out what was going on.

When Scott returned, he had a set of some sort of zip-tie handcuffs with him.

Why the hell had Scott brought those along? Dumb question. I knew why. He had been paranoid about bad guys and pirates, plus he was a retired cop. I might travel around with a spare credit card, in case something went wrong, Scott traveled with handcuffs.

I liked his approach much better just then.

Francine and I watched as Scott deftly constrained Janet's wrists behind her back with one set of those flexible little handcuffs, and then a second set on her ankles.

Janet wasn't about to go anywhere.

Dawn roughly pulled her up and forced Janet to sit on the large padded chair behind the puke-sodden helm that Sally and Tony were now working to clean up.

Having set the boat to motor along on its own, Charlie had retreated to the aft of the yacht. He still had more breakfast to unleash.

Another boat cleaning was imminent. Not by me, though. I would let Charlie have that lovely chore all for himself.

Also, for the first time ever, I was ecstatic over Charlie's propensity for seasickness. I was even imagining the custom sweatshirt I wanted to order and the yet-to-be-devised clever slogan. His puking had saved us.

While Charlie was losing the remnants of his breakfast, Dawn was attempting to interrogate Janet to find out what the hell was going on and what her game plan was.

Her answer was troublesome. "You'll find out," she gave an evil chuckle. "It won't take long now."

"What won't take long now?" Dawn grilled her.

"Others are coming for the emeralds and me. I called them before we left. See," she nodded to the port side of the boat.

I didn't see anything at first. Then I did. A midsize express yacht was racing toward us. That boat was a horrible choice for these waters. It was a low-profile yacht, much better suited for fast, short jaunts in the Caribbean or around Florida. Not in these rough northern waters.

I started to tell the others this, as we all looked out toward the approaching boat. Scott, who had been holding Janet while Dawn conducted the interrogation, moved toward the helm to retrieve a pair of binoculars from a cubbyhole.

That move saved him.

It did just the opposite for Janet. She died. A large caliber bullet through her head killed her instantly.

I think that bullet had been intended for Scott. If so, it had been a stupid move on the part of the bad guys. Scott and Janet had been so close to each other, and on a moving boat, that there was a good chance of hitting the wrong person. They had.

Another blast had struck Sally, severely wounding her on her shoulder. A few inches to the left and Sally would have been dead, as Janet now was. Sally had been saved due simply to the erratic movements of the boat on the rough water. Otherwise, that bullet might have killed her.

Francine screamed in terror as she looked down at the gore from Janet which now covered my wife's left side.

Charlie, our fireman and resident quasi-paramedic, rushed from the cockpit. His sickness immediately gone at the sounds of the shots and my wife's scream. I saw his professional nature and background takeover as he tended to Sally's wounds.

Scott looked out at the approaching express yacht and, with a grave look on his face, called out for us all to take cover.

Then all hell broke loose.

~ ~ ~ ~ ~ ~

39: Mayday

Rapid-fire shots were raking across *Trixie's Destiny*. Several hit nearby, shattering fiberglass all around us. I looked up to see the glass panel in the fly bridge cover shatter.

It was as if they knew that their compatriot, Janet, was dead. Perhaps they did. Otherwise, why would the firing have been so intensive? Or, maybe she was expendable.

That last thought was scary. If their own teammate, Janet, was expendable, what did that mean for us?

I glanced over to the oncoming speedboat as it roughly bounced over the waves and could see a man looking at us with a pair of binoculars. Yes, they now knew that Janet was dead or wounded. What we didn't know was if that was a big deal to them or not.

With bullets flying around us, we all worked our way down to the pilothouse as quickly as we could. Charlie carefully guided the wounded Sally down the steep stairs as Tony and Francine followed. Scott told them to go below and hide in the hallway which connected the three forward cabins. He wanted them in the place which was least likely to have a bullet come through and strike them.

I wondered if there was any place on this boat which would be safe from those high powered shells. I was doubting it.

We left Janet's body up on the fly bridge. At that point, we really didn't care what happened to her remains.

Scott yelled at me to take the controls and get us the hell out of there!

I quickly took the helm chair in the pilothouse and gunned *Trixie* to full power. We had never had this powerful yacht at max power before and I didn't know what she would do.

We lurched forward, gaining speed. Impressive for a boat that size, but it still wasn't enough.

I didn't know which direction to point our boat, except away from the bad guys. They were coming closer and the shots were increasing in frequency and accuracy.

The windshield to my right, next to where we usually ate, blew out!

I was focusing entirely on maneuvering *Trixie*, hoping that I wouldn't burn out the engines. We were going fast, over twenty knots, and the bumping over increasingly rougher water was jarring.

The only good thing about this was that if the rough water was making it difficult for us in this sturdy boat, it would be doubly so for the bad guys there in that light-weight speedboat.

With the air now rushing in through the blown out pilothouse window, I suddenly remembered to call for help. We were miles from anywhere, with no other boat in sight, so it was unlikely that anyone could save us, but I had to try.

I picked up the marine radio, not able to take the time to determine what channel I was on. Hopefully a good one. "Mayday! Mayday! We are under attack. Our position is approximately fifteen miles southwest of Annette Island. I repeat, we are under attack!"

I wanted to say more, but couldn't. Shots continued to hammer the pilothouse and I had to duck down. I held the wheel while crouching down, popping up only briefly to make sure we were weren't about to bump into anything.

Not that there was a whole hell of a lot to bump into out there in that open body of water.

I wanted desperately to find a safe haven to take *Trixie's Destiny*, but there was simply no place to hide. Instead, I chose to keep on a course out into the ocean. Maybe that speedboat of theirs would be unable to follow us further out. It certainly wasn't designed for that type of rough water. I briefly fantasized about the other boat being tossed over by a large wave.

Lacking any other plan, my goal was to head further into rough blue water, hoping it would help the situation. The problem with this plan, however, was it was taking us further and further from land and possible rescue.

Then, the cavalry came. It was in the form of Dawn and Scott brandishing semi-automatic weapons. They separated, with Dawn rushing to the aft cockpit, and Scott darting up to the fly bridge where the vantage point would be best. He would also be more vulnerable up there.

There was also that whole "floor completely covered in Janet's blood and gore" thing. Scott would simply have to take care to not slip in it.

Those weapons are loud!

Dawn and Scott were blasting at that offending boat, and the men who had been openly positioned in the bow and cockpit.

I think we caught the bad guys off guard. They'd found it easy to find and kill Roger Amund and Herbert Langton, and they probably expected we would also be easy prey.

They hadn't met the likes of Dawn and Scott.

I turned to look at the approaching speedboat, a forty or fifty-footer, just in time to see a guy die. I knew this because of Dawn's gleeful war whoop and the way that body went flying off of the other boat and into the cold blue water.

One down, a whole cartel or two of bad guys to go.

Tony then joined in. Scott yelled to him where to find another weapon, the very one that Inspector Gibson had found in the couch in the main salon many days before.

Tony, with weapon in hand, and having to maneuver as our boat thrashed about, worked his way up to the starboard side door, near where I was piloting *Trixie's Destiny*. Soon, only feet from me, a third weapon was pounding into the bad guys' boat.

It seems that Tony knew his way around weapons.

We were giving them a beating.

They were giving us a beating.

Our boat was getting hammered.

With the engines roaring, we chopped our way from swell to swell, heading deeper into rough blue water. All sheltered bays and channels were now well behind us.

My wife came up from the lower deck to join in, trying to hold steady as the boat slammed through the swells. Damn, that woman had moxie I never knew existed. I definitely needed to remind myself to never piss her off again.

Francine wasn't picking up a weapon as I had thought. What she did was much smarter: she'd thought to resupply ammunition for the others. Scott yelled down to her where she could find additional magazines. She got down on her hands and knees to avoid getting shot, crawled over to get more ammo from a drawer, and then crawled first to Dawn in the cockpit with a full magazine for her gun. With Dawn resupplied, my wife worked her way up the cockpit ladder, with the boat lurching about, to resupply Scott, and finally she went to help Tony who was the closest to me.

Just as she came to Tony, he was shot down!

Francine screamed again. Tony had fallen on her and he was bleeding profusely.

Luckily, Francine wasn't hurt. Unfortunately for the bad guys, my wife was pissed. She grabbed the weapon that had been Tony's and, without my knowing she had it in her, began blasting away at the speedboat, which had been holding back since we first went on the offensive.

She took out their engine! At least, I think it was my wife's shooting that did it. What I did know for sure was that right after she started firing, a burst of smoke belched out from their boat's cockpit area. My guess was that an engine was on fire and the smoke and flames were working up from the cockpit floor.

The speedboat came to a complete stop.

Scott yelled for me to stop as well. I hesitated. All of my gut instincts were yelling at me to get out of there. Instead, I did as Scott requested, but made sure *Trixie's Destiny* was a safe distance away from them first.

Francine immediately went to help Tony. He was in trouble. The only good was thing was that he wasn't dead, but he was bleeding something horrible.

Charlie, hearing that Tony had been shot, rushed up from his station below where he had been helping Sally. Again, he impressed me with his quick response and knowledge of what needed to be done.

He mashed a compress against Tony's abdomen and held it there as he and Francine moved his body over to the couch in the main salon. This was going to be close. Who knew what damage had occurred inside his body.

Then the guys on the speedboat waved a white flag!

I didn't know that anybody actually ever did that. They could have just called our boat on the marine radio. Thinking of this, I decided to make another call. We definitely needed the Coast Guard and I really didn't care from which country. For all I knew, *Trixie* could have been sitting smack dab on top of the boundary between the two countries.

I turned on the radio to make the second distress call. No luck. It wasn't working. I now wondered if it had been working when I had made that distress call earlier.

It looked fine there in the pilot house, but it wouldn't work. I guessed that the bad guys had killed our antenna and satellite with one or more rounds of fire. Soon, I knew they had. Our navigation equipment was also out.

This wasn't good. We couldn't communicate and we didn't know exactly where the hell we were. Rather like the good old days before cellphones were invented.

Now I knew why they were waving that white flag...probably someone's underwear or a piece of a sheet. Few people happen to travel with a white flag at the ready. They must have tried to call and then had found that we weren't responding. Thus, the flag.

Scott came down from the fly bridge but yelled out to Dawn to remain where she was and to keep her weapon trained on the other boat.

I told him that the radio was dead. He thought about this a moment and then told me to edge closer to them.

I did. Scott went to the forepeak with his weapon pointed steadily at them, while kneeling to keep a low profile and help keep steady.

"Take those bastards out!" Charlie called out. He was red-faced mad. They had shot two of our group, Janet had betrayed him, and our boat was Swiss cheese.

"I would love to," Scott responded, "but it would be like playing *Whack-A-Mole*. Take these guys out, and more like them would just pop up again."

I rather liked that analogy. I also agreed with Charlie. I too wanted to take the bastards out. Scott had a different opinion which, for a retired cop, surprised me.

"We need to find a way to make them go away forever and not want to kill us in the process," Scott called out to us. "This has to be solved now!"

I edged *Trixie* closer to the speedboat.

We could see three men standing on that boat with their arms raised in surrender. Even seeing this, I expected for them to suddenly start shooting at us again.

They probably would have, except for the menacing way Dawn and Scott were pointing their automatic weapons at them.

Then I heard Scott call out to my wife. "Go find every damn fire extinguisher you can. Bring them to the cockpit."

What did Scott want to do with the extinguishers? Was he planning on dousing them with fire extinguisher foam?

~ ~ ~ ~ ~ ~

40: Weapons Exchange

Bit-by-bit I brought *Trixie* closer. One hand was on the throttle and the other on the joystick. I was ready to get us the hell out of there if need arose.

Both boats were bobbing up and down in that rough water. One moment we would be looking down at them, the next, they would be at an even level with us or even above us. This movement kept us from being able to tie the boats up together. I kept a distance of forty yards. This way, there wouldn't be a chance that an errant wave would bash our two boats together.

Their fire appeared to be out. I saw a fourth man crawl out from an open hatch from the engine area, which was accessible through the cockpit floor. He had a fire extinguisher in his hand. Also, the smoke had lessened. Lucky for them, they had been able to easily put the fire out.

They had real fire extinguishers.

We seemed to have emerald-filled extinguishers.

"Are you dead in the water?" Scott called out to them.

He was playing nice with them now? Moments ago, we were all trying to kill each other. I didn't get it.

"I do not know. We will start our engines to test them, if you don't shoot!" One of the men, probably their leader, called out.

"Go ahead. I give you two minutes to check your engines. If you try to move an inch, you're dead," Scott announced.

Hearing this, and seeing Dawn and Scott direct their weapons at the men standing there, it felt like we were all in the middle of a bad gangster movie. The dialogue definitely had a familiar ring to it.

The others watched and listened for the engine. I watched and listened for trouble. I knew what I would do if need arose. Given the larger size of our boat, I could easily spin *Trixie's Destiny* to face them and then run that damn boat over!

It would damage our boat in the process, but Trixie was now already heavily damaged. I couldn't see how she could be patched up again. Bullet holes were everywhere. Running over a speedboat would just be the icing on the cake.

Soon, we all heard the sound of an engine and we waited for a moment. No smoke arose.

"One engine works, although not well. The other is dead," the bad guy called out. "We can get to shore."

"Good! Now get the hell out of here!" Charlie called out.

Scott shushed him. This, apparently, was not the way to handle this sort of situation. He would know. Scott had been decorated for bravery three times during his career and had handled more than one hostage situation.

"We want what is ours. The jewels," the man called out. "We mean you no harm."

"Yeah, we can tell by the wonderful bullet-laden greeting!" Charlie barked, again causing Scott to shush him. Charlie was definitely not helping the situation.

Hearing what they had said about only wanting the emeralds, I wondered. Could it be that simple? Could we just give over the emeralds to these guys, assuming we were right about where they were hidden, and then they would be off of our backs? I doubted it.

"We will trade you," Scott called out.

"We have nothing to trade," the man called out.

Scott clearly had a plan.

"Emeralds for weapons. First, you throw a weapon overboard, and we give you the body of your woman. Then, with each additional weapon, we give you a fire extinguisher. Supposedly all of the jewels are in them. Your woman seemed to think so."

"Your woman?" I mulled. That wasn't exactly politically correct, but somehow, it worked.

Scott continued. "We don't know which ones have the jewels. So we will just pick ones which seem likely. Then, when we are sure that all of your weapons are gone, we will give all of the remaining extinguishers to you."

This sounded like a good plan to me. No more bad guy weapons and no more damn emeralds.

"Oh, one last thing," Scott added. "For the last trade, you all have to go to the forepeak of your boat and stay there while one of my crew comes and searches your boat to make sure all weapons are gone."

"Your crew?" Charlie called out to Scott, clearly annoyed.

"Shut up, Charlie. Not the time!" This time it was Dawn.

"You can inspect the fire extinguishers before we part ways, to make sure you have all of your emeralds," Scott added. "We don't want for you to think we are cheating you."

He definitely seemed to know how to work with criminals like them. If it had been up to me, I would have rammed their boat by now.

The men on the boat talked amongst themselves. This offer from us was unexpected. As greedy as they were, and as greedy as Roger Amund and Herbert Langton had been, they weren't ready to believe that we were so ready to give up the emeralds.

"You can have every last one of them. Trust us. We want to cleanly part company," Scott called out, restating our intention, after seeing the hesitation on their faces.

Those guys knew that if they didn't get the jewels today, they, or others in their group, could come back at any time and finish the job. While we may have won this battle, they would eventually win the war if they wanted.

Attempting to cheat them could be deadly. If not today, then later.

Curiously, the loss of two of their team, the guy we shot off of the boat and Janet, didn't seem to faze them. I guess they just chalked that up to the cost of doing business. Their business spreadsheets were probably way different than any I ever crafted. I certainly had never built in a data column for "dead bodies" as a business expense.

Luckily, they didn't seem prone to want to have another battle. The trade took place and it took place pretty much as Scott had outlined.

The difficult part was getting rid of Janet's body after the first weapon was pitched into the water from the speedboat. Charlie and Francine took on the gruesome task of moving Janet's body. I would have helped, except I needed to be there at the helm with my hands on the controls.

It was a gruesome experience. Blood and gore from Janet's bloody head, and other fluids, ran onto Charlie and my wife. They don't show that sort of thing on the TV mystery movies. Eventually, they were able to place Janet into the speedboat's tender, which had been moved with difficulty by one of their crew over to *Trixie's* swim platform.

This done, Francine went to the far side of our boat and threw up. Unbeknownst to her, she had picked one of Charlie's favorite places. Charlie soon joined her, and together they created a formidable mess.

Then, one by one, they threw a weapon into the water, and we placed a fire extinguisher into their tender, alongside Janet's body.

Those people had a lot of weapons.

We had a lot of extinguishers.

Charlie was pissed and I couldn't blame him. He kept complaining about us wimping out and how we should blast the bastards.

Scott kept shushing him.

I silently agreed with Charlie. We had wimped out and this just didn't feel right. In every spy or detective novel or movie I had ever read or watched, the bad guys got it in the end. Not with us, we were about to let them head off on their merry way and with a boatload of emeralds.

This sucked.

They finally said that they were done. Scott had previously said that we would send one of us to their boat to check for additional weapons, but it was too dangerous. The water was simply too rough to allow any of us to get into a tender to take the trip over to, and then back from, the other boat.

They had done it, and we now had that tender with one of their crew tied up to *Trixie*, but they seemed to have had little concern for the low-man-on-the-totem-pole that they had sent over.

They only wanted one thing, their emeralds.

We wanted only one thing. To stay alive.

Scott ultimately decided to have their guy come aboard *Trixie* while we lashed that tender to our boat. Dawn then followed him about with a pistol pointed at him, as he looked through every cabin and closet to verify that no further fire extinguishers remained.

Finally, it was done.

We could see them open the extinguishers as they stood openly on the deck of their boat. Some were normal and filled with fluid or foam, and others appeared to have small packages tucked deeply inside them.

In the end, they yelled out that they had all of the jewels, and then turned their wounded speedboat away from us and limped back with one engine to their mother ship, or wherever they had come from. The key thing was that they had chosen to head northeast, back into Alaska. We chose a different direction and a different country.

Charlie didn't want to retreat, and he loudly complained, while he was close to tears. This whole event had been horribly wrong and, in the end, we had two wounded loved ones and a banged up boat.

With the bad guys heading away, we did a retreat toward Canada and none of us liked it. We wanted revenge but we also knew that was not likely to happen. We had to save Tony and Sally.

We wanted to go to Prince Rupert, and we wanted to get there as quickly as possible. I probably could have picked one of the many uninhabited islands as our destination, but we had two wounded people on our boat, and they needed help!

I had to weigh the options...go as fast as possible, knowing that the rough movements of the boat could be jarring to Sally and Tony, or go slower so that they would have an easier ride, but it would take longer.

Tony was in a bad situation. I chose to run up the engines to about three-quarters power and get us there quickly but not at full power, while crossing my fingers that I wasn't screwing up.

Without navigation equipment, it would be difficult, but I recognized a few of the mountains to the east. Seeing this, I knew there was a reasonable chance I could get us in the general proximity of Prince Rupert.

What I didn't know. What no one had known, even as we searched the engine room for more fire extinguishers, was that a small fire had started as a result of one bullet, and my firing up the engines to race toward Prince Rupert had made the situation worse.

Ten minutes after kicking our engines in gear and starting our mad dash toward the distant port, *Trixie* was ablaze.

Trixie's Destiny was on fire and all of our fire extinguishers were long gone!

Maybe there had been a flaw to Scott's plan after all.

~ ~ ~ ~ ~ ~

41: Trixie Down

The first I knew of the fire was when I heard Dawn's yell. That got our attention. Dawn is rarely excitable, so I knew something was wrong.

Then the smoke was obvious. It was taking over the main salon and making it hard to breathe. Even the wind rushing in through the shattered windows was not enough to lessen the smoke.

We had to get Tony out of there. He was horribly wounded and now he was at risk of smoke inhalation on top of everything else.

A few moments later, we were all at risk of being fried to a crisp. Flames were coming up from the engine and crew areas.

We had no choice. We had to abandon ship!

This was another area where I had to praise Charlie. He had made us practice fire and safety drills several times. The big difference was that we had fire extinguishers at hand when we did those drills. Now we had none.

One aspect of our drills was to do a quick launch of the tender. Normally when launching the tender, we would safely secure it to the crane and then carefully move the tender up and over until it was placed gently into the water. A fairly slow process. For this emergency, we took a totally different tack. Throw the darn thing overboard.

It worked. That tender, with its engine, is damn heavy, but with Charlie, Scott and me hefting it, we were able to quickly get the tender down from the fly bridge and into the water on the starboard side. Thankfully, it landed right side up.

In the meantime, life vests were gathered and everyone, except Tony who was too wounded to do so, soon had one on. Even Sally, with her wounded shoulder, was able to put on a life jacket, although I did hear her sob from the pain once during the process.

We then moved Sally from the hallway down below and got her into the tender. Tony was next. He cried out in pain multiple times as we quickly moved him into the waiting tender.

Francine and then Dawn quickly scurried into the bobbing tender, and then the rest of us followed.

We now had seven people in a tender meant for four, and one of those people, Tony, had to lie down. Sally, thankfully, was able to sit upright.

I fired up the small engine and gave thanks when it started. With the engine running, I turned our little craft away from *Trixie's Destiny*, so that we could get far away from danger.

This led us from one danger... fire, directly into another danger...an angry ocean. The swells, out there in that horribly cold water, tossed our tender about like it was a toy.

"Oh my, look!" Francine called out, and we turned to look at *Trixie's Destiny*, which was now in our wake. It was our last sight of that wonderful yacht. *Trixie* was fully in flames and, with all of the holes from the bullets, was rapidly taking on water.

As we slowly motored away, with the tender dangerously overloaded and water sloshing into our little craft, we watched *Trixie* die.

It took about five minutes for it to end. Our final view of *Trixie*, with us now about a half-mile away, was to see her go under.

It had been a great adventure learning how to pilot and manage that big yacht, and then taking her on the trip to Port Townsend, and finally this scenery-filled trip up to Ketchikan.

And, now that was all over.

We didn't have much time to contemplate the loss of our yacht. We had to stay alive. The only thing in our favor was that it was daytime, and we actually had our little tender to get us to safety.

"We have a leak!" I heard my wife exclaim, and I looked from the tiller to where she pointed. She was right. My guess was that a bullet had punctured the bottom ribs giving the tender a hole the size of a dime and water was gushing in.

Charlie rammed his thumb over that hole, reminding me of that old story about a boy putting his finger in the dike to keep it from flooding his Dutch town. In our case, Charlie's actions didn't stop the flow of water, but it helped.

I didn't know if we could make it. We had around thirty miles to go. It wouldn't be to Prince Rupert; that Canadian port was just too far away. Dundas Island, which stood between our position and Prince Rupert, was our new goal.

Thirty miles give-or-take a few. Maybe we could make it. With each passing second the water should be getting smoother and the passage safer.

My spirits lifted with the knowledge that we could be there within a few hours at the pace our tender would go. It wouldn't be fun, but we could do it.

The real big "if" here was if the amount of gas in the small tanks were enough to get us to our destination.

Then the rain started. It wasn't heavy, but it was cold and miserable.

Tony was shivering, so Dawn held him close and tried to cover him with her jacket.

Sally was crying and holding on to Scott who was doing everything he could do to comfort his wife, while he too placed his jacket over her.

The rain drenched us all.

How long would our little motor last? I didn't have a clue.

Then I did. It stopped. After an hour of motoring toward distant Dundas Island, our little engine died.

My spirits died right along with it.

~ ~ ~ ~ ~ ~

42: McDuck's Coffee Bar

It was good to be back.

Seven weeks later, and three of "the guys" had started to reconvene at McDuck's Coffee Bar on Thursday mornings. Just like we used to.

Everything was the same in some ways, and totally different in others. Somehow, I felt older and wiser, and I sensed that the others did too.

Our experiences had changed us.

I pulled into the parking lot that mutually bordered McDuck's on one side and the marina on the other. I worked my way around an overly large, new, converted bus that was parked in my usual spot plus two additional parking spots. It was one of those bus-RVs that cost more than a normal person's house. We see a lot of these monsters around Anacortes.

After pulling in, I got out and gazed wistfully at the marina. Without *Trixie's Destiny* there, that marina would never be the same. A Grand Banks motored by as I looked at the marina, a model similar to *Trixie*. When I saw that sturdy boat, it prompted me to reflect on the end of our adventure. It had been close.

After the motor on our little tender had died, we sat in that cold, rough water in freezing rain for quite a while, not knowing what to do.

Two common attributes among us were fear and more fear. Fear for our own lives as we sat out there in that cold, wet and miserable situation. And fear for Tony who looked near death.

Scott, Charlie and I had taken turns at jamming a thumb, a hand, a foot over the hole. Still, the water had been coming in. Another hour, and it was likely that the tender would sink.

Where was a role of duct tape when you needed it? Duct tape fixes everything, right?

With the tender gone, we would have only our life vests to keep us afloat and marginally alive.

Luckily, Charlie's penchant for "all things safety" saved us. He had placed a pack of safety gear in a built-in cubbyhole in the tender. In that packet we had: a knife…little help in our situation, granola bars…definitely helpful, a medical kit…minimally helpful…Sally's and Tony's wounds were beyond what help that little kit could provide, and three rocket flares with small parachutes.

That last item had saved us.

Dawn had been in tears as she watched Tony fade. That incredible, hard-as-nails former detective had turned totally to mush as she saw her guy so close to death.

Then, just as we were feeling like the end was near for all of us, Francine saw a boat in the distance, perhaps a mile away. There was no way they could see us, but we quickly pulled out one of the parachute flares and lit it, then watched it jet high in the wet, gray sky.

I had prayed that the rain wouldn't kill the flare or keep people on the boat from seeing it. It didn't...we just didn't know that for a while.

Several minutes later, we eventually realized that the boat, an Alaskan State Ferry, had turned and was heading toward us! Someone had seen our flare.

We were going to live!

I will remember that moment for the rest of my life. Watching that low profile, white-on-blue ferry come our way was one of the most beautiful things I had ever seen.

Sitting in our sinking tender, we watched as they rapidly dropped one of their own large lifeboats and motored over to us.

Ten minutes later, we were on the ferry, having left our tender to drift off and sink.

The ferry had been crowded with tourists and locals, all looking down to us in the water, pointing and taking pictures. That ferry system does an incredible job of servicing towns small and large, from Washington State up into many remote areas of the Alaskan coast. It was also a popular way for tourists to travel. Now it would also serve as a rescue ship.

We ran out of luck when it came to finding a doctor on board. I had hoped that, like cruise ships, this boat would have a resident doctor or nurse. No such luck. The ferries have first aid kits and nothing more.

The captain had made a quick decision after getting us on board and learning of Tony's condition. He had the choice of continuing on to Ketchikan or heading over to Prince Rupert. We were much closer to Prince Rupert and there was a small regional hospital there. This caused the ferry to be very late for its arrival in Ketchikan, but it was the best way to get Tony to the help he needed.

Two hours later, with Tony in a desperate situation and Sally in great pain from the bullet wound in her shoulder, we were in the hospital. An ambulance had been waiting for us at the port. Dawn had begged for a helicopter once we had boarded the ferry, but there simply was no place to land one on that ship.

After that, it had been a wait-and-see situation. Dawn and Scott had remained in the hospital as my wife, Charlie and I met with Inspector Gibson.

We had a lot to tell him, and the inspector and others in that station eagerly took down all of the information we could provide.

Soon, we were retelling the same story to more agencies from both the U.S. and Canada then we could count. This event likely took place in both countries, involved; murder, international trade, smuggling, and who knows what else. I stopped trying to keep track of the alphabet soup of agencies who wanted to grill us over and over.

Eventually it was done. At least, we hoped it was.

Our duty had been done, but I found myself hoping that Inspector Gibson would not pursue the bad guys. I had a feeling that we were okay as a reluctant gentlemen's agreement had been reached regarding the emeralds out there on the water.

That little agreement didn't set well with the numerous agencies we had to talk to. Screw them. They weren't out on the water having to make life-or-death decisions as we had been.

Further activity by the Canadian authorities might only make things worse, causing the Colombians, if they were Colombians, to want to come back to us for some sort of retaliation. I told this to the inspector, but given the deaths of Roger, Herbert and Janet, it was unlikely they would leave things alone. We could only hope that their work to resolve the murders would not bring us back into it. We definitely did not want to incur the wrath of those bad guys.

If the bad guys were pursued or not, a mystery remained. Why had they waited to attack us when we were up north? They could easily have broken into *Trixie* weeks before when she was docked in Anacortes. Scott thought that the answer might be that security cameras were all around the marina plus the local authorities back home were alert to things being amiss. Also, it would be easier for them out in the remote area where we had been attacked. Perhaps. Unfortunately, unlike all of the mystery movies where everything is neatly wrapped up at the end, we simply would not ever know why events unfolded as they did.

Those mysteries also didn't set well with the Canadian and U.S. authorities. I will bet that more than one of them thought that we were guilty as sin given our lack of good explanations. Why were we attacked where we were? Why did they just head out after getting the emeralds without trying to kill us? Why didn't we kill them? Did we catch any names? How many emeralds were there? Our answers were: I don't know, don't know, and, don't know. Again, screw them. Maybe one day we will figure out a few things, but for now all we had were actual facts and not enough of them.

Dealing with numerous authorities wasn't our only problem to solve while stranded in Prince Rupert. Arriving as we did, we had no ID, wallets, cellphones, passports, credit cards or money. We also didn't have any other clothes when we arrived, and we were soaked.

What we did have, was an amiable and helpful police inspector. Thanks to him, what could have been a huge hassle, turned out to only be a moderate hassle.

Walmart served as our new clothing store, with Inspector Gibson footing the bill. He also put us up in a local hotel for the duration, again with his agency footing the bill.

Scott's general paranoia had come in handy again. He had advised us all to make photocopies of our passports and drivers licenses, and even make a log of our credit cards, and then place all of that in a password-protected cloud account.

It worked. Using a computer in the hotel lobby, we were able to obtain all of the account info we needed, which helped incredibly in getting each agency to process replacements, even the passport agency.

It still took four days for everything to arrive to us. This was okay, we had the time. Until Tony and Sally were okay, we weren't about to leave that place until we knew that Tony was going to make it.

Sally, luckily, was out of the hospital two days later with her arm in a cast and sling. She was going to have to go through a lot of physical therapy, though.

Tony, who was in critical condition when he'd been brought into the hospital, took much longer and had to stay in the Prince Rupert Regional Hospital for almost two weeks.

The rest of us, except Dawn, didn't wait that long. We hung around a few days, but soon saw that Dawn was amply smothering her beau with attention. He didn't need the rest of us there.

So, we left Dawn and Tony there in that remote Canadian town and headed home. We obtained permission from a half dozen agencies to depart. With new passports, credit cards, wallets, and a few new clothes from the local Walmart, we took a charter jet that Charlie had booked for us.

That is definitely the way to travel.

Ten days later, Dawn and Tony were back as well, and Tony had been moved to a recovery center down in Everett. We had each made trips to see him there in the hospital. Finally, three weeks ago, he was released and was back home with his two sons. They had been staying with Tony's mother while all of this had been going on.

As I thought of Dawn and Tony, I had to chuckle. Talk about a change! The two of them were now engaged, and

Dawn had gone all "girl" on us. After announcing her engagement, she had made one attempt to suck us into helping her plan their wedding. No luck.

Discussing wedding dresses, flowers, caterers and such was definitely not our thing. Unless, of course, she wanted to wear Levis, hold the wedding at McDuck's, and serve McBeignets to the guests.

She didn't. So, Dawn was now my wife's new BFF and, together, they were having a great time working on the wedding details.

I think Francine may have found a new calling. She was great at this.

Dawn was also absent from our regular Thursday morning thing, but it was starting to look like Tony might join us. If so, we would actually be four guys.

One chapter in our lives was now finally closed. Charlie had received a hefty check from the insurance company. Receipt of this check meant that "all things *Trixie's Destiny*" were in the past. We didn't even have any of our Co-Captain's caps as mementos, they were all down at the bottom of that cold body of water. Or, who knows, maybe some of them popped back up to the surface. I hope so.

Life had definitely taken some interesting turns.

Putting my reminiscing in check, I turned away from the marina and the array of boats and headed toward the weathered front door of McDuck's Coffee Bar.

The smells there were wonderful. An acquired taste, certainly, but very welcome in an aged, burnt coffee sort of way.

"I'll have a stack of those new cranberry McBeignets," I called out to Mac who had disappeared into the back of his kitchen-laboratory.

After waiting a few moments, Mac came out and filled my order. With McBeignets in hand, I turned to face my two partners in adventure: Charlie and Scott.

"Guess what!" Charlie called out gleefully.

"I'm afraid to ask."

"I bought a new motorhome-bus-RV thing! It's sitting out front. Just think of the adventures we can have!"

~ ~ ~ ~ ~ ~

- - END - -

Please check www.BGPreston.com for details on other stories by B.G. Preston.

Your feedback and reviews are always welcome and encouraged.

~ ~ ~ ~ ~ ~